CLASS PICTURES

Something was different about Lolly in seventh grade, and whatever it was, I didn't like it. . . . Class pictures came late that year, and it was then, looking at Lolly's face in the picture, that I suddenly realized what it was that had been different about Lolly, and what it was that I hadn't figured out until just then.

Lolly had become a beauty.

"This is a story capitalizing on Sachs's ability to combine rugged humor and pathos."
—*Publishers Weekly*

Class Pictures

by MARILYN SACHS

PUFFIN BOOKS

PUFFIN BOOKS
Published by the Penguin Group
Viking Penguin, a division of Penguin Books USA Inc.,
375 Hudson Street, New York, New York 10014, U.S.A.
Penguin Books Ltd, 27 Wrights Lane, London W8 5TZ, England
Penguin Books Australia Ltd, Ringwood, Victoria, Australia
Penguin Books Canada Ltd, 2801 John Street, Markham, Ontario, Canada L3R 1B4
Penguin Books (N.Z.) Ltd, 182–190 Wairau Road, Auckland 10, New Zealand

Penguin Books Ltd, Registered Offices: Harmondsworth, Middlesex, England

First published in the United States of America by Dutton Children's Books, 1980
Published in Puffin Books, 1991
1 3 5 7 9 10 8 6 4 2
Copyright © Marilyn Sachs, 1980
All rights reserved

Library of Congress Catalog Card Number: 91-52533
ISBN 0-14-034682-1

Printed in the United States of America
Set in Baskerville

*For Sharon, Jan, Heather, Emily, Myra, Joyce,
Ellen, Todd, Ben, David and Monica,
whose friendships, hopes and class pictures helped me
to understand Pat and Lolly.*

Chapter 1

Lolly doesn't remember, but when we first met, I bit her cheek, and later she wet the ground.

It was in kindergarten, and Lolly says she can't remember much before third grade. Maybe it was because her earlier memories were so painful. Lolly seems to forget anything that hurts. Not me. I remember everything. And most of all, I remember the bad times.

Not that kindergarten was a bad time for me. When I look at my kindergarten class picture, I am proud of me as I was then. I am standing between Kenny Saxton and Maria Sanchez, and I am taller than either one. Kenny is smiling with his mouth open, too wide for a smile and not wide enough for a laugh. His eyes are blurred because just before the photographer snapped the picture, he shifted his eyes over toward me. He looks terrible, although Kenny was at his cutest in kindergarten. It was downhill all the way for him, starting with first grade. Maria is smiling a huge, deep smile. She is so proud to be standing next to the most popular kid in the class—which was me.

Lolly wasn't in the picture because she didn't start kindergarten until nearly Halloween. Her family had just moved here from Saint Louis. She hadn't started kindergarten in Saint Louis because her mother thought it would be easier for her to adjust to school if she started fresh in San Francisco.

Lolly doesn't remember any of this, but I do. I can remember everything about her and the day she first arrived in Mrs. Weedon's morning kindergarten class. I was playing in the doll corner with Robin Haller and Judy Lee. The three of us were lying on the floor making believe we were dead babies when Mrs. Weedon asked us to look up and meet a new classmate. Nobody was supposed to move because we were dead, and out of the corner of my eye I could see that both Robin and Judy were peeking.

"You're cheating," I hollered at them.

"Pat!" Mrs. Weedon said in her soft, little voice that turned up at the end. I left off glaring at Robin and Judy and looked over at her. Next to her stood Lolly and her mother. Lolly's mother was nodding and smiling the way grown-ups do when they are nervous. Lolly was holding on very tightly to her mother's hand and looking hard at me. I guess she didn't like what she saw because suddenly her lips began quivering and two fat tears rolled down her cheeks.

Everything about Lolly was fat then. She was wearing a blue-and-white checked dress with a red cat on one pocket. From under the dress, her pale white, fat

2

legs billowed down into white socks and red shiny shoes. I couldn't take my eyes off her. I had never seen anybody with a face like hers. It was pale white, except for her cheeks. Just looking at her cheeks made my mouth fill with saliva. They were large, round, and very red. Like apples. I loved apples in kindergarten. I still love them—especially those big, round, red McIntosh apples. And Lolly's cheeks looked like two shiny red McIntosh apples.

I stood up and moved closer, fascinated. Mrs. Weedon saw me coming and said encouragingly, "This is Patricia Maddox, Lorraine. She is one of the friendliest girls in the class. Maybe Patricia can show you around."

Up closer, Lolly's cheeks looked even more delectable than at a distance. Under the tears that still glistened on them, Lolly's cheeks shimmered like apples under water. I came closer.

When I tell it, it sounds as if everything happened quickly, but as I remember it, everything moved in slow motion. Even the voices of the adults are slowed down in my mind.

Very slowly the grown-ups spoke to each other as Lolly's eyes fastened themselves in terror on mine. She stopped crying and stood hypnotized as I approached, licking my lips. Above, there came the sound of adult laughter, but Lolly's anguish was written all over her face. I felt it, but could not understand her terror. All I could think of was the taste of apples.

"Now Pat," said Mrs. Weedon, "why don't you show Lorraine where we put our clothes, and . . ."

But I struck then. My teeth fastened themselves on one of Lolly's cheeks, and Lolly screamed.

3

I didn't scream and I didn't cry, but I was bitterly disappointed. The cheek didn't taste anything like apples. It didn't even taste good.

Roughly I was dragged away and shaken by Mrs. Weedon. "Why?" she wanted to know. "Why?"

I could not explain, so I was told to sit down at one of the tables and lay my head down until I could behave. I kept my head down a long, long time. My disappointment was unbearable.

Even though I couldn't see anything, I could still hear. Lolly yelled for a while. Her yells sounded like hiccups. In between yells she said very clearly, "I want to go home! I want to go home!" I was miserable because now I understood that look of terror in her eyes and I realized that she was right and I was wrong. I felt humiliated and I hated Lolly. I put my hands over my ears to drown out the sound of her voice.

Later, Mrs. Weedon came over to my table and sat down next to me. I couldn't see her because I still had my head down on the table but I knew she was sitting there.

"Pat," she said.

I buried my head deeper in my hands.

"All right, Pat," she said.

Keeping my head down, I managed to move my body away. I wanted to show her that I didn't like her anymore, and I had liked her very much up until that day.

"You can sit up now, Pat."

I shook my head. No.

"Pat," came Mrs. Weedon's voice, "It's no good biting. If you are angry, you have to find some other way to show it. If each of us went around biting people who made us angry, we'd all be full of holes."

4

I felt the tears rising in my eyes. How wrong she was! How unfair!

I sat up. "I wasn't angry!" I yelled at her. "I wasn't."

"Then why did you bite Lorraine?" she asked, looking at me, puzzled.

I couldn't tell her. Now I realized how silly it was. Here I was, a big girl of five years old, as my grandmother was always reminding me—mixing up cheeks and apples. How could I tell her?

"I wasn't angry," I said.

She didn't press the point, and I was allowed to rejoin my classmates. Lolly now was one of them, and I kept looking over at her with hate.

"Silly pig face!" I said to Robin about Lolly, and Robin laughed.

"I bet she has cooties," I told Karen Stein.

The feeling was definitely anti-Lolly as the morning progressed. Mrs. Weedon kept moving Lolly from one group to the other, her bright, cheerful voice encouraging kindness. But none was forthcoming.

We all went out to the yard at recess to practice the dance our class was going to perform for the parents during the Halloween party. Everybody had been working on a scary mask—some of us were ghosts or witches or devils. We were going to stand in a circle and sing our spooky song:

> Lock your doors on Halloween
> Spooky shapes can then be seen
> Don't dare stop us as we fly
> We will scare you if you try
> Whoo! Whoo! Whoo! Whoo!

We would be wearing costumes with our masks while we sang our song. Then, at the *whoo*s, all of us would break into a dance where we whirled around each other and flitted back and forth across the circle.

It was while we were standing in the circle and singing that it happened. Mrs. Weedon didn't like the way the song sounded the first time we sang it. She couldn't hear the boys, she said. It was halfway through the song the second time—I can remember I had just finished singing *Don't* and was about to sing *dare* When I saw Richie Kronberg suddenly stop singing and point. "Look!" he cried.

Everybody looked. Some looked and continued singing, while others looked and stopped singing. In any case, the singing had stopped completely by the end of the line. Nobody sang anything after *fly*.

Richie Kronberg was pointing at Lolly. She was standing in the circle just like everybody else. Her mouth was even shaped in a circle as if she had been singing. But we knew right away that Lolly had been doing something else because down on the ground a long, dark, narrow stream moved quickly out from between Lolly's legs toward Susie Holmes who stood next to her.

Susie leaped up and fled.

"Look what Lorraine did, Mrs. Weedon. Look what she did!"

Everybody looked except for Lolly. She was trying not to look, and her whole face now was red, not only her cheeks. It made me feel better seeing all of her face red—not only her cheeks. Because now I knew for sure there were no apples there at all. It was just a red face—a sad, humiliated red face.

"Baby!" somebody snickered.

"I bet she has cooties," Karen said to me.

Lolly stood inside a ring of laughter, and she shuddered. It made me angry, suddenly, seeing her stand there, humiliated. It evened the score. I didn't hate Lolly anymore. I knew how easy it was to make a mistake. We had something in common.

I broke out of the line and hurried toward her.

"Pat!" I heard Mrs. Weedon warn.

Lolly put her hand up as I drew near. On her left cheek I could see very plainly two small horizontal marks. In her eyes I could see the same look of terror.

"I'll show you where the girls' room is," I told her and I took her hand.

That's how we became friends.

Chapter 2

Lolly's birthday was on August 27th, and mine was on October 14th.

Mrs. Scheiner, Lolly's mother, complained a lot about it. She made it sound as if somebody was to blame because Lolly's birthday fell in the summertime before school started. Sometimes when she said October was a "perfect month" and looked hard at me, I almost wondered if maybe it was my fault.

"The boys always had wonderful parties," she told me. "Michael's birthday is in December, and when he was small, I sometimes took all his friends to an ice-skating rink. Greg's birthday is in May, and if the weather was good, I always planned a cookout party. But Lolly—poor Lolly has always been cheated. None of her little friends were ever around on August 27th. But this year," said Mrs. Scheiner, "it's going to be different."

Mrs. Scheiner worried a lot about Lolly. She was always there after school, ready to pick Lolly up and drive her home. She never sat inside the car and waited for Lolly to find her, as most of the other mothers did. She stood right inside the yard, the first mother you'd see as the class came out of the building. She'd smile and wave, and after a while some of the kids in the class began waving back at her even though she was only waving at Lolly.

Lolly tried to make her wait in the car but she never would.

That year, when we were in first grade, school started on September 8th. On September 9th, Mrs. Scheiner came into our class in the morning, carrying a large white box. Inside the box were twenty-six cupcakes, one for each child in the class. Some were white cupcakes, frosted with white frosting, some were chocolate, and some were pink. Each had an *L* in silver candy balls on top and one little pink birthday candle.

I knew Lolly's birthday was in August, so I looked around at her, surprised. But she was grinning from ear to ear, and when Miss Bauman told her to come up to the front of the classroom so everybody could look at her when they sang "Happy Birthday to You," she scampered up as fast as she could. It was hard to say who had a bigger smile, she or her mother. She was dressed up, too, in a frilly new yellow dress with daisy buttons and sleeves like flower petals. So she must have known.

"But your birthday was in August," I told her later.

"I know," she said, "but my mother wants me to really celebrate this year. Please, Pat, don't tell anybody."

I promised I wouldn't, and then Lolly said, "I'm not supposed to say anything—even to you—it's supposed to be a surprise—but you're going to find something when you go home today."

"What?" I asked her.

"I'm not supposed to say," she said, watching me and waiting for me to ask.

But I acted like I didn't care. Lolly hated it when I acted like I didn't care.

"Don't you want to know?"

I shrugged my shoulders.

"Pat, don't you?" Her round, rosy face pleaded with me.

"I don't care."

"Oh Pat, listen Pat, it's a letter. It's an invitation to my birthday party. It's a costume party, Pat, and it's for lunch and there's going to be presents for everybody."

My invitation was waiting for me when I arrived home. Grandma was slicing cabbage for coleslaw on the kitchen table. Right in the middle of the cabbage and carrots and mayonnaise was that day's mail, including a pink envelope with my name on it—Miss Patricia Maddox. There was a little piece of grated carrot over the *r* in Patricia and several shreds of cabbage just below the stamp.

"Grandma," I yelled, "you're getting cabbage all over my letter."

"Well, get it out of here," said my grandmother, impatiently. "I keep telling you not to leave your things lying around."

I took it into the living room, opened it up, and saw a little Dutch girl smiling at me and holding out an invitation, on which there was another little Dutch girl smiling at me, holding out something too small to distinguish. Inside there was a lot of writing. I could make out Lolly's name—*Lorraine*—but nothing else. So I took it back to Grandma and asked her to read it to me.

Grandma put the knife she was slicing cabbage with down on the table, examined the invitation, and told me I was invited to a costume lunch party for Lolly this coming Saturday at noon.

"Grandma, can I go over to Lolly's house now?"

"Can you take Joey and Bobby?"

"Do I have to, Grandma? They always run around and climb over everything, and Mrs. Scheiner gets sore."

"How about just Joey?"

"He's the worst, Grandma. Please, Grandma, can't I go by myself for a change?"

Joey and Bobby are my kid brothers. At that time, Bobby was four and a half, and Joey was three.

"How about just Bobby?"

"Please, Grandma! Please! Just by myself, and I won't stay long. I'll come back and take them both outside. Please?"

Grandma sighed, resumed slicing cabbage, and I hurried out of the house before she changed her mind.

I lived on Sacramento Street, over the carpet store, only three blocks away from Lolly's house on Washington Street. Somewhere in between, the neighborhood changed. As soon as I stepped off the curb of my street, I left all the stores behind me; and as I moved from Clay Street to Washington, the houses grew wider, the streets cleaner, and the people more fashionable.

I was allowed to cross streets by myself, but Mrs. Scheiner always made me get into her car after school and drove me home. She didn't like it that I was allowed to cross streets by myself, but she never exactly said so. A few times she asked me if my mother knew that my grandmother let me cross streets all by myself. When I told her yes, her mouth moved down and her eyebrows moved up.

Lolly was crying when I got to her house, and Mrs. Scheiner was on the telephone, talking in a high, very excited voice.

"What's the matter?" I asked Lolly.

"It's Diane Frost and Karen Stein. They both called up and said they couldn't come to my party, and now I bet Jill Wong won't come either. She always does whatever they say."

". . . Well, I'm sorry to hear that," Mrs. Scheiner was saying. "Lorraine will be very disappointed. She was looking forward . . ."

"Who's your mother talking to?"

"To Karen's mother."

Mrs. Scheiner put down the receiver.

"What did she say, Mommy? What did she say?" Lolly's nose was running, and she didn't even bother to wipe it.

"Well, it sounds as if Karen and Diane were planning to go shopping with Karen's aunt, and . . ."

Lolly started screaming. She lay down on the ground and screamed and kicked her feet up and down. "*I'm* coming to the party," I said in a loud voice, but her screams were too loud, and I guess she didn't hear me.

"Now Lolly." Mrs. Scheiner sat down on the ground and tried to pick Lolly up.

"*I'm* coming," I said in a louder voice.

"You see, Lolly," said Mrs. Scheiner, "Pat is coming, and I'm sure all the others will come too. Seven is a very nice number for a party."

Just then the phone rang again, and Lolly stopped screaming. Mrs. Scheiner stood up, walked over to the phone, and, even though she arrived there after the second ring, let it ring a third time before picking it up.

"Hello. . . . Yes? . . . Just a moment, please." She held out the phone and said, smiling to Lolly, "It's for you, dear."

Lolly heaved herself up, sniffed a few times, and took the receiver. "Hello? . . . Yes . . . yes . . . yes . . . Good-bye." She put the receiver back, lay down on the floor again, and resumed screaming and kicking.

"That must have been Jill," I whispered to Mrs. Scheiner. "But don't worry, I'll fix it."

I didn't stay long that afternoon because I had promised Grandma I would be back early, and because Mrs. Scheiner said maybe it was better if I went home.

So I collected Joey and Bobby at home and set out for Karen's house. She was really the ringleader, I figured, and I knew how to deal with her. Karen lived over on Clay, just a few blocks away. She answered the doorbell and smiled when she saw me. Everybody liked me in the first grade.

"Come in, Pat," she said.

"I can't," I told her. "I've got Joey and Bobby with me."

"They can come in too," she said. So we all went inside.

"What do you want to play?" she asked me.

"I don't care," I said. "But why aren't you coming to Lolly's party?"

"Oh, Lolly!" She made a face. "I don't like Lolly. I don't want to go to her party. Besides, my aunt is taking me shopping for a new coat, and we're going to have lunch at the Hippo."

"If you go to Lolly's birthday party," I told her, "I'll invite you to mine. But if you don't go, I won't invite you."

"Are you going to have a birthday party?"

"Sure I am, but I won't invite you if you don't go to Lolly's. I won't invite anybody who doesn't go to Lolly's."

After that we played with her dollhouse for a while, but then her mother came in to say that Joey and Bobby were having a water fight in the bathroom, and why didn't the three of us go home.

So all ten children who were invited came to Lolly's party. She was dressed like the Dutch girl on her invitation, and her red cheeks stayed red all afternoon. It was the fanciest birthday party I ever went to, and the quietest. There were china dishes on the table, and all sorts of choices for lunch—chicken or roast beef or ham. The mashed potatoes were molded up into flowers and each child had a pear salad with carrot-stick arms and legs, nuts for eyes, and a cherry mouth. The cake was shaped like a ballet dancer and the ice cream was served in little, pale pink fluted dishes.

Later there was a piñata filled with candy and presents for all of us, and a magician who came and did tricks.

I came as Pocahontas. I wore my bedroom slippers, and Grandma cut up an old brown apron of hers and put fringes all over it. I wore two sea gull feathers in my hair under a red hair band, and a few strands of Mom's beads. Grandma combed my hair into two braids, and let me climb up on the chair in her bedroom so I could see all of me in the mirror. I looked good. Even Grandma said so, and she gave me a quick, dry little kiss on my nose.

Grandma said I could only spend a dollar fifty for a present for Lolly, but I talked to Mom and she gave me an extra fifty cents. She even came with me to the dime store and helped me pick out a toy doctor set. It was a good idea since Lolly's father was a doctor, and her two older brothers wanted to be doctors too. Sometimes Lolly said she wanted to be a doctor but other times she said she wanted to be an actress.

After the party was over, Mrs. Scheiner gave me two extra party cups of candy for Joey and Bobby, and a large hunk of cake out of the ballerina's skirt for my whole family.

I told my mother and grandmother when I got home that I wanted a birthday party.

"Where?" asked my grandmother. "Here?"

Here was our small four-room apartment over the carpet store.

"Why not?" said my mother. "She never had a party. I think it would be nice if she had a party."

"Who's going to do the work?" my grandmother wanted to know.

"I will," said my mother.

But the day of my party, which was a Saturday, Mom was still asleep when I got up. She worked as a waitress, and sometimes she didn't get up until the middle of the afternoon. Grandma said I shouldn't wake her. She gave me some money to go and buy Kool-Aid.

"What about candy?" I asked her.

"Do you have to have candy?"

"It's a party," I said. "Everybody has candy at a party."

Grandma said it was no good for children's teeth to eat candy, but she gave me another dollar.

"What about a cake?"

"I'm baking a cake." Grandma looked grim. That was bad news because Grandma generally baked either one of two cakes—a lemon cake or a marble cake. I didn't like either one.

"What kind of cake?"

"A chocolate."

"Chocolate?" Grandma had never made a chocolate cake before. It made me hopeful. What you don't know about might turn out good just as well as bad.

"Can you make it look like a ballet dancer?"

Grandma snorted. "If I'm lucky, it'll look like a chocolate cake."

"How about ice cream?"

"Do you have to have ice cream?"

"Mom said I could have ice cream."

Grandma gave me another dollar. She slammed her purse closed very hard and began muttering to herself, so I figured there was no point asking her about party decorations. I bought a half-gallon of marble fudge ice cream in Safeway and spent half the candy money for lollipops and half for M & M's. I bought orange Kool-Aid and had enough money left over for a package of napkins that said *Happy Birthday* on them.

When I got back, Mom was up drinking coffee. She said she would make the Kool-Aid, but then she said she had to go to work today and was afraid she'd have to miss the party. Grandma was filling a big pan with gray-colored batter, and she just grunted when Mom said she had to leave early.

"You know what?" I said to her. "We have to have presents."

"You will," said Grandma. "I guess your friends will bring presents, but I don't want you asking for presents when they come in. And remember to say thank you."

"No, Grandma, not presents for me. I mean for them. We have to have presents for them."

Grandma put the cake pan in the oven and turned around and looked me over. She didn't say anything. She just looked. That always meant stop it.

"Everybody does it at parties," I explained to her. "Nowadays you have to give each child who comes a present. Like Mrs. Scheiner gave me a ball-point pen with five colors."

"And Joey wrote all over the walls," said Grandma. "Forget it. And besides, I'm all out of money."

But Mom said she had an idea. I could give the girls some of her old junk jewelry.

"And what about Scott Dillon and Kenny? I'm going to have two boys at the party."

Mom said not to worry. She'd think of something. She gave me a hug and a kiss and called me her birthday girl. In those days, Mom didn't seem to mind me so much.

So I went and poked around in her box of junk jewelry. She was always buying new stuff and getting tired of the old. When I was real little, I thought she must be very rich. I picked out a jingly yellow coin bracelet for Lolly and some pins and necklaces for the other girls. Mom found a box of rubber bands for Scott and a comb that was hardly used for Kenny.

I had forgotten to buy birthday candles, so when Grandma brought in the cake, it had only one white

17

candle in it, which was disappointing. So was the cake, which tasted as bad as Grandma's lemon or marble cake. Maybe it even tasted worse.

But the ice cream was good, and so were the lollipops and M&M's. Everybody seemed to like their presents. The girls put on the jewelry, Kenny went around combing everybody's hair, and Scott shot rubber bands all over the house.

Grandma said why didn't we all go outside to play—and take Joey and Bobby with us. Most of the other kids weren't used to playing on the street but they didn't mind. We all had a good time. We played hide-and-seek, dodge ball, Two Square, Mother, May I? and Red Light, Green Light. Scott and Karen said they had more fun at my party than they ever had at anybody else's party in their whole lives.

Some of the mothers weren't too happy, though, when they came to pick up their kids. Mrs. Scheiner especially wasn't happy. After my party she never wanted Lolly to play at my house. She said to me that she preferred having me come play at Lolly's house, where there always was adult supervision.

I told Grandma, and Grandma said that it suited her just fine having me play all the time at Lolly's house. And that if Mrs. Scheiner wanted to supervise a couple more kids, she could have Joey and Bobby too.

That year the class pictures were taken in February. I am wearing the pink sweater that Lolly gave me for my birthday. By February, it had a tear on the left side of the collar which you can see if you look carefully. Lolly's hands are folded in her lap, and she has the coin bracelet that I gave her on my birthday on her left wrist. We are sitting next to each other and, even seated, you can see how much taller I was than Lolly.

We look so different in that first-grade picture. I am tall and thin and very dark, and Lolly is short and fat and very fair. Her blonde hair is in soft curls all over her head while my long, dark hair is pulled back in two ponytails. Karen Stein is sitting next to me on the other side. Many of the kids wanted to sit next to me in the first grade, but I picked her.

Chapter 3

In second grade I discovered who I really wasn't. It was because of Mrs. Scheiner, and for a while I hated her and stopped playing at Lolly's house. I know she felt sorry because after I came back, she used to go out of her way to talk to me and say nice things about me. As I grew older, she approved of me and encouraged my friendship with Lolly. Sometimes I think to myself that maybe Mrs. Scheiner was the real reason I became what I am today. Maybe, in the long run, she was the best friend I ever had. Maybe. But I can never really like her. There are too many sore places inside me that will never heal because of her.

If anybody ever made me feel awkward and sloppy and poor, it was Mrs. Scheiner. Whenever I came home with Lolly after school, her eyes would travel all over me. She never said anything, but often she'd tell

Lolly that *her* sweater looked messy or that *her* jacket needed washing. Nothing ever looked dirty or messy on Lolly, although Mrs. Scheiner was forever fussing over her. I knew there were buttons off my jacket, and stains on my sweater, and scuffs on my shoes—but I only knew it because of the way Mrs. Scheiner fussed over Lolly and looked silently at me.

She wanted Lolly to play with some of the other girls in the class—the ones who also lived on Washington or on Clay. She particularly tried to get Karen Stein and Lolly together, but Karen hated Lolly when we were small. She tried to get Diane Frost to play with Lolly too, and Kim Carpenter and Lisa Goodman. Nobody could stand Lolly then, and if I weren't her friend she would have suffered much more than she actually did. It was only when I was absent from school that they'd dare to torment her.

Why? I think about it and wonder why we became friends. We were always so different, but the differences fit into each other when we were together. It made me feel good to look after Lolly and protect her. She was grateful to me for that and she admired me for my courage and my popularity. But Lolly could do things I couldn't. She drew beautiful pictures—in the second grade, it was houses and families. She could put me into any kind of house I wanted and give me any kind of family I described. Once I lived in an igloo with an Eskimo family and I wore a white bearskin hooded jacket and carried a harpoon. Another time she put me on a ranch—she put us both in that picture. We were sisters and we lived out in the country, in a house that had rooms that looked like stables, with a black horse for me and a palomino for herself. I didn't think the horses looked too good but I didn't mention it. And Lolly was funny, too—she could imitate people's voices and the way they moved and walked. She could imitate her mother and my grandmother. She could imitate me. Sometimes I'd start laughing when Lolly got going and I couldn't stop. Sometimes in school all she'd have to do was raise one eyebrow and twist her mouth around in a funny way, and I'd be off. A few times, in second grade, Miss Wu had to send me out of the room to pull myself together.

Nobody else thought Lolly was funny in second grade. What most people saw was a fat, timid little girl who cried a lot and was no good at Four Square or dodge ball.

I was absent when they took the class picture in the second grade. I had an upset stomach and a fever. There are lots of teeth in that picture and lots of holes where teeth should be. The faces look small but the teeth seem enormous. Lolly is standing between Lisa Goodman and Robin Haller. Both of them are shrinking away from her as if she had the bubonic plague. She is smiling a particularly hearty smile, displaying a large gap in her lower teeth. She is trying to look happy, as if she didn't realize that both Robin and Lisa hated to have her near them. When I look at that great big smile on Lolly's face I know how miserable she must have been feeling, and even now, even after all these years, I hurt inside to think of it.

We were at her house one afternoon, sitting in the breakfast nook in the big bay window of the kitchen. Mrs. Scheiner always had cookies and milk for Lolly when she came home from school, and if I was with her, there were cookies and milk for me too. That afternoon there were chocolate chip cookies, and I had been wolfing them down. By second grade, I was expected to pack my own lunch and sometimes, like on that day, I forgot. Mrs. Scheiner had been questioning Lolly about her day's activities as she always did, and I took advantage of her interest in Lolly's achievements to dispatch one cookie after another.

Halfway through my seventh cookie, I realized that Mrs. Scheiner was looking at me. I slowed down my chewing, wondering whether I should put back the eighth cookie, clutched in my hand under the remains of the seventh, or hope that she hadn't been counting.

"Do you know what I'm thinking, Pat?" she said.

I had a pretty good idea, so I put back the eighth cookie.

"I'm thinking," she continued, "that you don't look at all like your mother."

I picked up the eighth cookie and bit into it.

"I saw you both together at the market the other day. You didn't notice me, I suppose, but it really struck me how little you resemble your mother."

"Everybody says that," I told her, swallowing the last bite of the eighth cookie. Hopefully, I regarded the plate, but no cookies remained there. "I'm so dark and she's so light."

Mrs. Scheiner smiled. "That sounds familiar, doesn't it, Lolly?" she said. "Everybody's always saying how different we look from each other. Lolly's so fair, and I'm so dark."

"They're all light in my family except for me. Joey has red hair, but Bobby and my mother are blonds. Grandma's all gray now, but she used to be a blonde too. All of them have blue eyes except for me."

23

"I suppose you look like your father."

I considered what Mrs. Scheiner had just said, and thought about Daddy's picture on the bureau. Daddy had died when I was three, and I could hardly remember him. I mean, I remembered him but not his face. "My grandma says I look just like her father."

Mrs. Scheiner said, "I was thinking of your coloring. You'd have to get that from your father, if your mother's side is so fair."

"I think my father was fair too. I think he had blond hair and blue eyes."

"No, dear," Mrs. Scheiner corrected. "He would have had to have dark hair and dark eyes. If you have dark hair and dark eyes, your father had to be dark."

"But Lolly is fair, and you're dark and so is Dr. Scheiner."

"That's different," said Mrs. Scheiner. "Dark people can have fair children, but fair people can't have dark children."

"I don't see why not," I told her. "It doesn't seem very fair."

Mrs. Scheiner laughed kindly. Whenever Mrs. Scheiner laughed that way, I always felt particularly awkward and stupid. "You're too young to understand, Pat. When you're older and you study about genes in biology, you'll find out all about it. But in the meantime, dear, take my word. Your father *had* to be dark-haired and dark-eyed."

"I have a picture of him," I insisted.

"And—what color is his hair?"

"Well, it's a black-and-white picture, but it looks like he's blond."

"It's probably the way the light is hitting it. Black-

and-white pictures are often deceptive. But you go home and ask your mother. I'm positive that she'll tell you that your father's hair and eyes were dark."

"What color was Daddy's hair?" I asked Mom before she left for work that night.

"Blond."

"And what color were his eyes?"

"Sort of a gray blue."

"Were they brown?"

"I just told you they were blue."

"Are you sure?"

"Sure I'm sure."

Next day after school, I came home first, picked up Daddy's picture, and was nearly out the door when Grandma said, "Where are you going with that picture?"

"I want to show it to Mrs. Scheiner."

"Why do you want to show it to Mrs. Scheiner?"

"I just want her to see it."

"Well, be careful with it, and don't lose it."

I looked at the picture on the way over to Lolly's house and felt really happy. Mrs. Scheiner thought she knew everything, the big show-off. Well, she'd see she didn't know everything when she looked at Daddy's picture. Even though it was only black and white, his hair looked almost white and his eyes were much paler than his eyelashes. Big mouth! I couldn't wait to show her the picture and see how embarrassed she was going to look.

She certainly did look embarrassed. She studied the picture a long time while I told her several times that my mother said he'd had blond hair and gray blue eyes.

"And when did your father die?" she asked me.

"When I was three," I told her. "He was in a car accident. A policeman came around in the middle of the night and rang the bell and woke up my mother. I wasn't up. I mean, I missed it but she told me."

"I see," said Mrs. Scheiner. That's all she said, and it wasn't enough.

"He was blond and he had gray blue eyes," I insisted stubbornly.

"Yes, dear, I'm sure he did," said Mrs. Scheiner. But she said it in a funny way, and she quickly started talking about something else.

Grandma was sitting with her feet up in the living room, sipping a beer, when I returned home. Grandma's feet were puffy and covered with blue veins. The doctor told her she had to get off her feet as much as possible. She told him if *he* had to take care of three children under ten and one child under thirty, he'd come up with some other kind of treatment. But every afternoon from five to five-thirty, Grandma managed to sit down, elevate her feet, and drink two beers.

I brought Daddy's picture over to her and said, "Grandma, Daddy had blond hair, didn't he?"

"He sure did," Grandma said. "Very light, almost white. I always used to say to your mother, Kathy, I never saw a man with hair like that. It almost looked dyed. He certainly was a good-looking man. Bobby looks just like him, but I don't think his hair will stay so light."

"Mrs. Scheiner thinks she knows everything," I told Grandma. "She said Daddy had brown hair."

"How come she said that? She didn't know him, did she?"

Grandma lifted her first can of beer all the way up

and drained the last drop. Then she opened the second can.

"No, she didn't know him but she said he had brown hair and brown eyes."

Grandma chuckled.

"She said he *had* to have brown hair and brown eyes."

Grandma took a few deep drinks from her second can. The wrinkles in her neck moved back and forth.

"She said two people who have light hair and light eyes can't have a dark-haired, dark-eyed child. But she says dark people can have a light child. She thinks she knows everything."

There was foam above Grandma's mouth. She laid down her beer and looked at me.

"That's why I took Daddy's picture to show her," I laughed. "She didn't say anything when she looked at Daddy's picture. I guess she felt stupid for a change."

I began laughing, but Grandma wasn't laughing. She leaned back in her chair, closed her eyes, and looked like she was sleeping. I put the picture back on the bureau.

Next morning, Grandma said I should come home after school. "Why?" I asked. "Just come," she told me. "Your mother wants to talk to you."

"But Lolly and I were going with her mother to buy some tropical fish."

"You'll go another time. Today I want you home."

They were both sitting there in the kitchen, waiting for me, when I arrived home—Mom and Grandma. They were looking at each other and Grandma said to Mom, "Go ahead, Kathy, tell her."

"Tell me what?"

"Oh, it's no big deal," my mother said. She was all

27

made-up as if she was going to work, even though it was only two-thirty, and she had the night shift. She was even dressed, and her hair was combed.

"Well, tell her," ordered my grandmother.

"What?" I cried.

"It's just that I guess I never got around to telling you that—well, Pat, it's not so important but I—I was married before I married Daddy. I married somebody else and he—well, it didn't work out."

"I didn't know that," I said. "Lonny Price's mother married three times, and some of the other kids have parents who are divorced. Wait until Lolly hears this. Can I go now, Mom?"

"I guess so," Mom said, getting up.

"No, not yet," said Grandma. "Go ahead, Kathy, tell her."

My mother sat down again. "Well, Pat, it's just that—the first man I married, it didn't last, but we were married. Just remember that when you tell . . ."

"Kathy," warned my grandmother.

"Well, he was your father," Mom said sulkily and began smoothing her fingernails.

"You mean Daddy wasn't my father?"

Grandma took it up from there. "No, he wasn't your real father, but he loved you just as much as he did the boys. It was no different to him. He was just as good to you as he was to the boys."

I sat down. "Why didn't you tell me this before?"

Mom shrugged, and Grandma got up and began sweeping the floor. It wasn't often that she swept, so I knew she was turning cranky. But so was I.

"What was his name?"

Nobody answered, so I repeated it, my voice high and angry. "What was his name—my father?"

28

"Uh . . . Eddie," said my mother. "Eddie Rice."

"And was his hair brown?" I cried. There were tears rolling down my face now.

"I guess so," said my mother.

"And were his eyes brown?" I howled.

"Well, yes, they were," said my mother, "but that's nothing to yell about."

For the first time in my life, I dropped to the floor and began screaming and yelling and kicking my feet.

"Will you stop that?" screamed my mother.

"I told you to tell her years ago," yelled my grandmother. She scooped me up, pulled me into her lap, and nestled me against her shoulder.

I lay there yelling and shaking in fury. My grandma held me and patted my back and didn't say anything.

"I didn't think she'd mind so much." I heard Mom's voice out there. "Listen, Pat, you want to pick out something nice in the toy store? Up to five dollars. Pat, come on, we'll go to the toy store."

I looked at her, my face blazing with fury. "SHE said my father had brown hair and brown eyes," I shrieked. "SHE was right. SHE was right."

That was the worst part of it. I didn't go to Lolly's for a couple of months, and when I did, I never said anything to Mrs. Scheiner about my real father. I stayed home that afternoon and my grandmother played cards with me—Steal the Old Man's Bundle and War. The next day, I went to the toy store with my mother and got her to buy me a Barbie doll with two outfits. It cost more than five dollars, but she didn't complain at all, and I figured she owed it to me.

Chapter 4

Lolly remembers that day at my house. It was one of the best days we ever spent together. First of all, her mother wasn't around to "supervise." Her mother was home, sick with the flu. That was why Lolly was permitted to walk home with me after school and spend the afternoon playing at my house. Her older brother, Greg, was going to pick her up at five and walk her home. Even though Lolly was eight years old at this time, her mother still didn't let her go most places by herself. Especially on a winter afternoon, when it was half-dark by five o'clock.

It was a rainy day, an indoor day. Grandma was waiting nervously for us when we arrived home. She was even wearing a clean apron in honor of Lolly's visit, and the house looked as if she'd made an attempt at straightening up.

There were Oreo cookies to eat with our Kool-Aid

instead of the usual graham crackers. Grandma hovered over us. Whenever Lolly said anything to her, she'd smile agreeably but at the same time try not to show too much of the inside of her mouth, where two of her side teeth were missing.

"Aren't you going to tell your grandmother what Mr. Evans said to you today?"

Grandma looked at me, startled.

"Oh, it doesn't matter."

"Sure it does. Mrs. Hartman will want to know what he said. Won't you, Mrs. Hartman?"

I was not in the habit of sharing my school experiences with my family the way Lolly did with hers. I could see Grandma growing worried so I said, "Forget it, Lolly."

"No, I won't. I'll tell her. Mr. Evans said he thought Pat was a real whiz at math. He said she always finishes ahead of everyone else, and she's always right."

Grandma looked relieved. Bobby was in first grade by this time, and his teacher, Mrs. Flume, was forever sending notes home saying how bad he was. "That's nice," she said.

"And did Pat tell you what he said yesterday?"

Grandma sat down at the table with us and listened while Lolly rattled off first all the relevant school details about me over the last few days, and then about herself.

After a while, Grandma said hopefully that maybe we'd like to watch some TV.

"Lolly isn't allowed to watch TV during the week. And besides, Grandma, I promised to show her all our family pictures."

A long time ago, before Grandma had married Grandpa, she kept her pictures neatly in two albums.

But ever since then, all our pictures had been tossed into boxes. The pictures in albums were old—some of them went back to the turn of the century and were of Grandma's grandparents. There were pictures of Grandma as a little girl with her brothers and sisters, and later, pictures of her as a young woman with pointy shoes and a short, wavy haircut. In 1938, Grandma married Grandpa, and the last picture in her second album is their wedding picture. She really looks beautiful, even better than Mom, in a long, white, satin gown with a train and a pearl tiara on her head.

"It belonged to a friend of my sister, Harriet," Grandma told us. She was sitting down next to us with her glasses on.

"You look gorgeous, Mrs. Hartman," Lolly said. "You must have been really beautiful."

"Well," Grandma laughed, "I always thought my sister, Harriet, was the real beauty of the family, but some people said . . . ah . . ." She studied her picture, and patted the hinges that held it on the page. "It was a long, long time ago. . . ."

"Tell us, Grandma, tell us about it."

I had heard Grandma's story about her wedding many, many times. Grandma enjoyed telling stories about her youth, and I loved listening to them.

"Oh . . . Lolly doesn't want to hear about an old woman like me."

"Oh please, Mrs. Hartman, tell us."

"Well, you know, Pat, my father was working as a conductor on the Southern Pacific line, and he didn't make a lot of money. There were eight of us in the family, so at first when I decided to get married, he thought we should have a small reception at home after the ceremony in church. But there was this passenger, Mr. Braddock. He used to take the train up to San Francisco from Burlingame every day. I guess you never heard of him, but he was a very rich man, and he owned a big fancy restaurant up on Nob Hill. Well, he used to have fits sometimes—he'd just fall down and start foaming at the mouth. Lots of times it happened right on my father's train, and then my father always took care of him. He'd loosen up his collar and put a pencil in his mouth so he shouldn't bite off his tongue. So he and my father became very friendly, and I guess my father must have told him about me getting married—I was the oldest and the first one—and Mr. Braddock told my father that he was giving me a present for my wedding—and the present was a reception at his restaurant. Oh—I'll never forget it. There were musicians—and a violinist, too—and flowers on all the tables, and oh, the food—it was so beautiful! Poor man, he died the next year. All that rich food, I guess. But it was a lovely wedding, even though somebody spilled wine on the gown. I had it cleaned but Harriet's girl friend made a big fuss. Harriet was mad too, because two years later, when she got married, Mr. Braddock was dead, and she had to have the reception at home."

We looked at Grandma's albums and then we looked at the pictures in boxes. My aunts and uncles when they were children . . .

"I don't know why I never got around to putting them in an album. I guess I was just too busy. We both were working in the store, and right away I had five children to look after. . . ."

"Maybe Pat and I could put them in albums for you, Mrs. Hartman."

"Now here, look at this one of your mother, Pat, with

33

your Aunt Mary and Aunt Barbara. Aren't they cute? People used to stop me on the street and tell me they looked like dolls. . . ."

"Who's this, Grandma?"

"That's your Great-uncle John, Grandpa's brother, and his wife, Hennie, and their two children."

"And who's this, Mrs. Hartman?"

We looked at pictures for an hour or so while the rain beat outside at the windows and the TV set hummed in the living room where Bobby and Joey were watching.

There were pictures of us as babies and a picture of Mom marrying Daddy. "It was a small wedding," my grandmother said. "They didn't want a big wedding."

Mom is wearing a suit with a corsage of flowers pinned to it, and Daddy is holding her hand and smiling at her.

"Where is a picture of Pat's real father?" asked Lolly.

Grandma took off her glasses and looked at Lolly for a moment the way she looked at me when I was getting on her nerves.

"That's right, Grandma," I said. "I never saw a picture of him. Didn't they take a picture when they got married?"

"Of course they did," snapped my grandmother.

"Well, where is it?"

"I guess he took it," said my grandmother. "I certainly don't have it."

We were getting tired of looking at pictures, so Grandma let Lolly and me rearrange the canned goods in the kitchen cabinets. They were never in any special place, and I loved to move them around. Sometimes I put all the same colors together, and sometimes the same sizes. Other times I played mix and match. Lolly built a bridge, with the tomato soups on top and the corned beef hashes for posts.

Mom came in around four. She'd been out looking for a new job and she was drenched.

"What a lousy day I had," she said, coming into the kitchen. "One lousy break after another." Her hair was plastered down on her head, and her mascara was streaming in dark streaks all over her cheeks.

Grandma took her dripping umbrella and told her to get into some dry clothes. "And this lousy raincoat," said my mother, "it's full of holes. I need a new one, and there's no lousy money."

"Hey, Mom," I said cheerily, "look, here's Lolly."

"Oh yeah! Hi, Lolly," said Mom and squished off to the bedroom.

We spent the whole afternoon in the kitchen. After we finished arranging cans, I got my marking pens, and Lolly said she would draw some paper dolls, and then we could dress them. First she drew me.

"Don't put my hair in ponytails," I told her. "I want to wear a hair band and have it flowing down my back."

Quickly, from under Lolly's hands, a girl appeared who looked just like me. She had dark brown hair, large, dark eyes and red cheeks with a very red mouth.

"She looks like she's wearing lipstick," I said.

"She is," giggled Lolly and made the lips even redder.

Lolly sketched in a short pink leotard over the girl's middle. Then she asked, "What kind of clothes should I make?"

"An astronaut's suit."

"I don't know if I can draw that."

"I have a picture in my library book."

While I was cutting out the paper doll of me, Lolly studied the picture in my book about space travel and began drawing. She drew me a green helmet with a part to cut out where the glass was supposed to be. She drew me purple space boots and purple gloves. My suit was in two parts. The jacket was a deep red and the pants were blue. The oxygen tank and pipes coming out of the jacket matched the blue of the pants.

Then she drew herself with blonde, curly hair, blue eyes, and a pale blue leotard. I didn't say anything but she made herself a lot thinner than she really was.

"What are you going to wear?"

"You'll see."

While I was cutting out the Lolly paper doll, Lolly drew a pink ballerina's outfit with pink ballet slippers and a pink crown.

"I'm going to take ballet lessons starting next week," she told me. "One day I'm going to wear a costume like that and dance in a real ballet."

"When are you going to take ballet?" I asked guardedly.

"On Thursdays."

"Thursdays!" I exploded. "You go to the dentist on Mondays, and on Wednesdays you take art lessons at the de Young, and now you'll be taking ballet on Thursdays. I guess I'll never get to see you."

"That's right," Lolly said, wrinkling up her face. "It was my mother's idea. She gets nervous if I have too much free time. But I'm not going to do it. I don't care about the ballet slippers and the tutu. If I take ballet, it would make three days we couldn't play, and I couldn't stand that!"

I smiled lovingly at her, but she didn't notice. She was busy drawing another paper doll.

"Who's that?" I asked.

"You'll see." I knew it was a grown-up because the body had breasts and hips and wore a bra and panties. At first, I couldn't identify the face. It had blonde, wavy hair, blue eyes, and a big smile.

"Who is that?" I asked again. "I give up."

"Just wait until I make her clothes. Then you'll know."

I began cutting out the doll while she drew a long white, satin gown with a lacy train.

"It's my grandma," I shouted.

Lolly drew a pearl tiara and pointy shoes trimmed with pearls.

"It's beautiful," I told her. "It's the most beautiful thing you ever drew."

"Now I want to draw just one more, and then I'm through," she said.

"Who, Lolly, who?"

"You'll see." Lolly hummed while she worked, and another grown-up with blonde hair and blue eyes appeared on the paper. But this time I knew who she was. "It's Mom," I said.

Lolly drew a bright red, shiny, new raincoat for Mom with black, crinkly boots, a red-and-white polka dot umbrella, and a red rain hat.

Suddenly it was a quarter to five. I couldn't bear for Lolly to go, and neither could she.

"Ask your grandma if I can stay for dinner," she whispered, and I hurried out of the kitchen before my courage failed me.

Mom and Grandma were together in the bedroom. Mom was complaining and Grandma was grunting in reply.

"Please Grandma, can Lolly stay for dinner?"

"No," said Grandma.

"But why, Grandma? I've eaten at her house lots of times, and she's never eaten here. And twice Mrs. Scheiner took me out to a restaurant."

"Didn't I just say no?" Grandma looked hard at me as if she was going into one of her cranks.

"Oh, let her stay, Ma. For God's sake, why shouldn't the kid have a friend over once in a while?"

"And what are we going to give her to eat? A child like that is used to the best."

"Grandma, we can have some canned spaghetti. Lolly said she never had any canned spaghetti while we were playing with the cans. And she loves spaghetti. And there's a can of peas and carrots, and some baked beans . . ."

"And where are we going to eat? It's enough of a squeeze with the five of us around the kitchen table."

"One more won't make any difference. Please, Grandma, there's canned applesauce and we still have cookies for dessert, and Lolly was crazy about the grape Kool-Aid."

"Oh, let her stay, Ma," said Mom.

Grandma began grumbling, but I knew that meant yes, so I said cheerily, "Thanks, Grandma, thanks a lot. I'll take the laundry over to the laundromat for you Saturday if you like, and Lolly will call her mother right now and ask her."

At first, Lolly's mother said no, but Lolly made such a fuss, crying and even yelling over the phone, that both Bobby and Joey left off watching the TV to come into the kitchen and listen.

"She said I could, and that my father will come for me at seven-thirty," Lolly gasped when she hung up the phone. Her lips were still trembling, and there were tears in her eyes and red splotches on her cheeks. But I began to laugh and so did she. We hugged each other and danced around the kitchen until Grandma came in and said we should set the table.

It was a tight squish, but Lolly ate everything on her plate and had seconds on the spaghetti. Grandma said it was a pleasure seeing a child eat like Lolly and that she wished I ate like that, instead of always picking at my food. She and Lolly really seemed to hit it off. After dinner, Grandma sat down with us at the kitchen table and admired the paper dolls Lolly had drawn. She held the paper doll of herself and kept putting the wedding gown on and off it. Lolly finally asked her if she'd like another outfit for the doll.

"Well," said Grandma, "I don't have a picture of it, but there was a fancy dress I used to wear—but I don't have a picture of it."

"What did it look like?" Lolly asked.

I brought her paper and pens again, and as my grandma described it, Lolly drew a bright red, low-cut dress with a jagged hemline edged with black beads. There was also a long strand of black pearls to fit over the doll's head.

Grandma cut the dress and the beads out herself and told Lolly that she used to love clothes and once when she was very, very young, she had thought about becoming a fashion model.

"You never told me that before, Grandma."

"I guess I forgot all about it myself until today." She told Lolly about a green pleated dress she had with a dropped belt and a little white collar, and another one, a yellow silk dress with puffed sleeves and lace trim down the front.

The doorbell rang, and Lolly said she'd promised

her mother that she would go right down when her father rang the bell, so he wouldn't have to come up. She thanked my grandma for the "delicious" dinner and promised to come back another day and draw the green pleated dress for her and the yellow silk.

As long as she stayed with us, Grandma kept the paper doll of herself and the wedding gown. She kept it in her jewelry box along with her mosaic butterfly pin, her strand of pearls, and the gold locket with Grandpa's picture inside. Maybe she still has it.

In our school picture that year, Lolly and I were separated because Mr. Evans had all the tall people standing in the back and the short people sitting in the front. Each teacher had his or her own way of arranging kids for class pictures. Naturally, Lolly and I liked it best when we were allowed to stand next to each other. Lolly looks terrible in our third-grade class picture. Her eyes blinked and she has a particularly moronic smile on her face. I don't look too bad, towering over Kenny Saxton on one side and Wayne Price on the other. In the third grade, I was the tallest kid in the class, the best at math, and teacher's pet besides. I am smiling a very wide, self-satisfied smile. Of all the class pictures, it was in the third grade that my smile was the happiest.

Chapter 5

They separated us in fourth grade. Lolly was in Mrs. Nagamine's class and I was in Miss Coleman's.

I asked Miss Coleman if I could be traded for somebody in Mrs. Nagamine's class but she said no. She said I should be pleased that I was in her fourth-grade class because it was a special class for special people. It didn't look very special to me. The only kids I knew were Kenny Saxton, Diane Frost, and Robin Haller. And there was nothing special about them.

Mrs. Scheiner was impressed. "You're in the gifted class," she told me.

"I don't want to be there," I said. "I want to be in Mrs. Nagamine's class."

"Both of my boys were in the gifted program," Mrs. Scheiner said. "Both of them were identified in the first grade." She made it sound as if they were some kind of freaks from outer space.

"It wasn't my fault," I told her. "I didn't do anything."

Mrs. Scheiner looked at me, puzzled. "I had no idea, Pat . . . but of course, it's not always apparent."

I felt as if I had soup stains down the front of my shirt and dirty fingernails.

"I didn't do anything," I said weakly.

"No, no, dear, it's nothing you can help," Mrs. Scheiner said. "It just means that you are a very intelligent person, more intelligent than most people. Only two percent of the population are as intelligent as you. And that's something you should feel very proud of."

"So why do I have to be in Miss Coleman's class instead of Mrs. Nagamine's?"

"Because you are in a class with other gifted children, children who are also very intelligent, and you'll probably have more complicated work, harder books—a more challenging curriculum."

It didn't sound like much fun. "I'd rather be in Mrs. Nagamine's class. Her class always does the Mexican Hat Dance for the May Festival, and she's always taking her kids on field trips."

Mrs. Scheiner continued to look curiously at me. "I really had no idea, Pat, that you were so . . . so . . ."

"Mr. Evans said Pat was a whiz in math in third grade," Lolly said, "and she reads a lot—hard books, too."

"Reads?" repeated Mrs. Scheiner.

"Not as much as I used to," I said apologetically. "Now that I'm sleeping in the bedroom with my grandmother and my mother is out in the living room, I can't stay up as late as I used to. Grandma says too much reading at night is bad for the eyes."

Mrs. Scheiner stopped looking at me and started looking at Lolly. "You see," she said to Lolly, "if you'd do a little more reading and a little less daydreaming, maybe you'd be in the gifted class too."

"I don't like to read," Lolly said.

"That's very apparent," said Mrs. Scheiner coldly, "and that's one reason why Pat is in the gifted class and you're not."

"I'd rather be in Mrs. Nagamine's class," said Lolly, "but I wish Pat was with me. The kids are so mean when she's not around."

After that, Mrs. Scheiner never seemed to object to our friendship. Suddenly her cool scrutiny of me changed to warm approval. She always asked about the work our class was doing and about the kinds of books I liked to read. On my ninth birthday, she gave me C. S. Lewis's *The Lion, the Witch and the Wardrobe.* I didn't tell her I had read it back in the second grade, and had finished all of the other Narnia books in the third grade.

I was no longer the tallest person in my class in the fourth grade. A boy named Christopher Moore was. He is standing in the center of the back row in my class picture. All the heads go downhill on either side of him. I am next to him on one side, and Kenny Saxton is next to me. I don't look happy. It is the first class picture in which I am smiling with my mouth closed—a poor, weak, little smile with no teeth showing. Kenny is wearing glasses and his neck looks long and skinny.

How I hated that class! I didn't feel special at all in that class. In the third grade, Mr. Evans always had time to talk to me and kid around. But Miss Colemman was always harried, always looking over your head while you were talking to her, always reminding you when you didn't do the homework or got the wrong answers that "You're too intelligent to get away with that kind of work." Nobody was really special in Miss Coleman's class. We were all the same—too "gifted" to be special.

I told Mr. Evans that one day in the yard. He was watching his new third-grade class playing kickball, but he smiled when I came over to him, and pushed his elbow out at me and said, "Here's my ugly duckling. What's up?" I knew I was special to Mr. Evans.

"I hate my class," I told him. "I hate Miss Coleman. I hate being gifted—and it's all your fault."

"My fault? Why is it my fault?"

"Because you took me down to the board of education last term when my grandmother couldn't go. That's when that smiley lady with bad breath gave me those tests and you took me out for ice cream later. If it wasn't for you, I wouldn't have turned out gifted and I'd be in Mrs. Nagamine's class with all my friends."

"You are one goofy kid," said Mr. Evans. "Miss Coleman is not exactly the life of the party, but you'll learn a lot more with her than with Mrs. Nagamine. Just give it a chance."

"I gave it a chance, and I hate it."

"Just be patient. It's time you learned to stretch a little."

"But suppose I keep hating it."

"You won't."

"But suppose . . ."

"Look, kid, get lost, will you. I've got my own problems."

He grabbed me by the neck, shook me fiercely, and pushed me hard away from him. I really was special to Mr. Evans.

Lolly didn't have to go to the dentist anymore on Mondays. She had bands on her teeth now and she spit when she talked, but her Mondays were free. Not for long, though.

"What's wrong with Girl Scouts?" Lolly asked.

"It's just dorky," I told her. "Who wants to wear uniforms and sit around with a bunch of giggly girls and eat cookies?"

"Well, that's what you and I do when we're together," Lolly protested, "and besides, they do other things too. They learn about art and hiking and cooking—and you get a badge for each new thing you learn about. My mother is going to be the scout leader, and she says we can go on camping trips, and maybe boating and horseback riding. . . ."

"No thanks."

"Come on, Pat, it would be such fun to be together in a club. I don't get to see you on Wednesdays because of my art lessons or on Thursdays because of ballet, and . . ."

"Well, whose fault is that?" I snapped.

"My mother makes me," she said weakly.

"No she doesn't," I told her. "You're always blaming her but you're really the one who likes to join clubs and take courses."

"Don't be like that," Lolly said. "How do you know you won't like Girl Scouts?"

"I know," I told her.

"But how?"

"I just know, and if you want to do a lot of things without me, that's your business."

"If it's a problem with money," Lolly said carefully, "my mother says you can get a second-hand uniform or maybe the troop can . . ."

"I don't want to join," I yelled at her, "and it isn't a problem with money, so shut up and leave me alone."

Sometimes on Monday afternoons after school, I'd watch Lolly and a few of the girls in her class dressed in their green uniforms, waiting in a group to be picked up by one mother or another. They'd be standing out in front of the school, a little green clump of them, their bright badges glowing on their chests. I'd hear them laughing and talking as I went by and avoided the pleading look in Lolly's eyes. Sometimes I enjoyed making believe I was excluded because I was poor and unwanted. Sometimes I could even work myself up to a fury of self-pity.

Although I complained bitterly to Lolly, I really was relieved to have Mondays, Wednesdays, and Thursdays free. On the other days, Lolly and I still played together, mostly at her house, and sometimes on Saturdays I could tag along if Lolly and her mother went shopping or to the movies. It was Lolly's world that I fit into, and in a way I loved that world as I loved Lolly.

But more and more now, I needed time to myself when I could be me. I was never a joiner, never really jealous of the clubs and courses Lolly was forever involved in. I needed my time free—especially in the fourth grade.

Grandma didn't let me read late at night now that I was sleeping with her in her big double bed. And she didn't always like it if she saw me home reading in the afternoons. She said I should be out playing. So more and more, I spent at least one or two afternoons a week over at the library. There was a spot behind the magazines where nobody ever bothered me. I'd settle myself in for a long read and finish one or two books before they closed the library and the librarian said I had to go home.

Blinking my way back into the real world, I'd float home, my eyes, ears, and brain still tingling from my reading. I read fantasies, sicence fiction, and space travel. They ran together in my mind and let me run free inside a wonderful blurry universe with no margins. I was at the center of all my books—they were written for me and about me.

Other days I wandered—on the street, to the playground—wherever my fancy carried me. Rainy days I might stay home reading or watching TV with the boys. Occasionally I might even go over to Kenny Saxton's house and play with his model trains or his toy dinosaurs.

It was always me on my free days, and I needed to be me after the bondage of my fourth-grade class. Looking back, I suppose Miss Coleman didn't really hate me the way I thought she did. Maybe it was only because she was neutral, not like Mr. Evans, whose likes and dislikes were apparent to the whole class. In Mr. Evans's class, everybody knew I was one of his pets and Richie Kronberg was not. Even when Miss Coleman yelled at Kenny Saxton for always jumping up and talking out, you knew she didn't dislike him any more than she liked Robin Haller, who always said the right things and sat in the right places at the right time. Even when she told me in a frosty, carefully controlled voice that I was wasting my time and the class's time as well by fooling around instead of working on the vocabulary exercises, I knew then she didn't really hate me. She liked us all the same or disliked us all the same—and I couldn't stand it. There was a sameness to that class. It was like being caught in a net with a bunch of fish exactly like yourself—and never being able to get free.

I asked Grandma to go to school and get me out of that class. Grandma refused.

I asked Mom. She was working at Zim's now on Van Ness. She said no, too. She said she was glad I was smart and that maybe I'd have a better life than she did. She said she only hoped Joey and Bobby turned out smart too, but the way Bobby was carrying on now in second grade, she wasn't too hopeful. She said she was having pains in her knees from too much standing and that her left elbow was hurting her. She thought maybe she had an arthritic elbow, and she just hoped she could keep working. She started crying when she said that—and I told her not to worry. I decided not to ask her to come to school again.

I waited for Mr. Evans one afternoon. Just stood outside his classroom and waited. He came out, grinning with his hair in a new curly style and wearing one of those embroidered work shirts, with a necklace of teeth around his neck.

"You look like a hippie," I told him.

"You look like a cockroach with a stomachache," he told me and yanked one of my pony tails. "What's up?"

"I have to talk to you."

"Well, make it fast. I'm meeting someone." He kept on walking, and I followed along behind him.

"Who?"

"What are you—an owl?"

"Listen, Mr. Evans, you've got to get me out of that class."

We were out of the building by this time. Parked in front of the school was a small, dusty Volkswagen. A young woman with a big bush of rusty hair stuck her head out of the window and yelled, "Jason!"

He smiled and nodded at her, then looked at me as if he was trying to remember what I was talking about.

"Who's that?" I asked him. "Your girl friend? Why doesn't she comb her hair?"

He started laughing, pulled me by my arm over to the car, and said, "Here, Meg, here's one of the main reasons I'm about to lose my sanity."

"Hi," I said to her unpleasantly. In spite of her messy hair, I couldn't help noticing that she had large blue green eyes, a soft, fair complexion, and white, even teeth. She displayed every one of them in my direction. "Hi!" she said enthusiastically to me. I took a complete dislike to her.

"Well?" I said, turning to him. "Are you going to do something? You promised you would."

"I never promised anything," he said, opening the door of the car.

"Yes you did. You said I should give it a chance and if I didn't like it, you'd get me out."

"I never . . ."

"Yes you did, you did!"

"What's the problem?" asked Meg, directing a sympathetic look in my direction which I found particularly irritating.

"This dumb kid," Mr. Evans said, sliding into the car seat next to her, "is in a gifted class and doesn't want to be there. In spite of her manner and style, she is a very sharp cookie but doesn't like anybody to know it."

"Well, I don't blame her," said Meg with one of those cutesy little pouty lip movements. "I was always the smartest kid in my class too and I hated it. All I ever wanted was to be cute."

Mr. Evans was looking at her, and she was looking at him, and nobody was looking at me.

"Well, I don't want to be cute," I shouted at both of them. "I just want to be me."

Mr. Evans came up for air then and said, "Look, Pat, I have to go someplace now, but come and talk to me tomorrow after school."

"That's right, Pat," said Meg. "Don't give up, and meanwhile, I'll give him a good talking to. I'm on your side."

I ignored her, nodded at him, and ran home. The next day, I came to see him after school, and we talked for a long time. After that, I waited for him sometimes on Wednesdays, and once he and Meg drove me home. Another time, I walked with them around Stow Lake in the park, and another time we all drank tea at the Japanese tea garden. I grew to like Meg in spite of the fact that Mr. Evans was really gone over her, and I stopped moving away when her arm rested on my shoulders.

I had to stay in the gifted class for all of the fourth grade, but in the fifth, I was back with Lolly and I was free again. I knew Mr. Evans was responsible.

Chapter 6

Lolly came down first with chicken pox in fifth grade. I told Miss Wertheimer that I would bring the homework assignment over to her house.

"You'd better not come in," Mrs. Scheiner said, "since you've never had the chicken pox." She stood in the doorway of the house, smiling but blocking my way. "It's very nice of you to bring the work over, Pat, but poor Lolly is feeling so miserable, I doubt if she's going to be up to anything very ambitious for a few days."

"I'm going to get it too," I told her. "Lolly took a bite of my sandwich yesterday, and Diane Frost is sick with it too, and she's in my reading group."

"You just might be lucky and not come down with it," said Mrs. Scheiner, "although it is highly contagious."

Mrs. Scheiner didn't understand—I wanted to get the chicken pox. I very seldom got sick with anything. Other kids had the flu or pneumonia or the mumps or even sore throats. The lucky ones broke arms and legs and wore casts, but in all my years of school, I had been out only three or four times, mostly with upset stomachs. Of course, Grandma never let anybody stay home unless they ran a high fever or were chucking up all over the place.

Every day I looked at myself in the mirror.

"See, Grandma, see these spots."

"What spots?"

"On my face. Don't you think it's chicken pox?"

"Now just don't go talking yourself into anything, Pat. The last thing I need is to be stuck indoors with you and the boys for a couple of weeks."

A few days passed and nothing happened to me. I spoke to Lolly on the phone every day. She said she had spots all over her, even inside her mouth. She also said her mother bought her a matching pair of pajamas and robe, a new set of marking pens, and some beads. Her father gave her two puzzles and her brothers bought her *Mad* magazine and a Glen Campbell record.

"Gee, I wish I could see you," I told her.

She said I should come by her house the next day after school, and she'd look at me out the window. But that afternoon, during art, I suddenly felt very cranky. I was working on a painting of a Viking ship with a high dragon prow, and it seemed to me that the dragon looked more like a sheep. I scribbled on it with a purple marking pen and glared over at Peter Balunsat, who made a face at me.

"Drop dead!" I told him.

Rosie Lee began giggling.

"Drop dead!" I told her too.

"Miss Wertheimer, Miss Wertheimer, Pat told me to drop dead. And she told Peter to drop dead too. And she scribbled all over her painting."

I glared at Miss Wertheimer as she approached our table. She was glaring back at me—Miss Wertheimer always gave as good as she got. But when she arrived, instead of telling me off, she hesitated, peered into my face, and then put her hand on my forehead.

It was a wonderful moment in my life. I had the chicken pox.

"I have the chicken pox," I told Lolly over the phone. "I'm running a fever of 101 and I don't have any spots yet, but I'm sick. I'm really sick."

"Oh, that's wonderful," Lolly said. "We can talk to each other all day long, and I guess I'll be able to come and see you when I'm better. My mother says I can go out in a couple of days. Once you've had it, you can't get it again."

But the next day I was too sick even to talk to Lolly for a few moments. I was sicker than I'd ever been in my whole life. Grandma kept coming in and out all through the day, bringing me Kool-Aid and water. She left the door open to the living room so I could see her or hear her whenever I was awake. Most of the time I slept, and when I was awake it was like being on an escalator which was either coming from or going into sleep. Far away in the distance I could hear Bobby's or Joey's voice and always Grandma saying, "Shh! Shh!" or "Go away—you'll wake her."

Once when I woke up, Mom was sitting next to the bed, and when I opened my eyes, she smiled a big, wide smile at me and bent over and kissed my forehead. I could smell the Dentyne chewing gum inside her mouth.

Another time I was dreaming that my arms and legs were made out of stone and I couldn't move them. When I woke up, Grandma and Mom were washing me off with alcohol. I was lying naked on the bed with towels all over and under me. It was so funny being washed off in bed that I started giggling. Grandma had such a worried look on her face that it made me laugh out loud. But my throat was so dry it didn't sound at all like my voice, and it hurt. Suddenly I was crying.

"You're going to be fine, sweetheart," Grandma crooned.

I kept drifting in and out of sleep. I never could stay awake for very long. Even when the doctor came. It was the only time a doctor ever came to our house. He was putting his cold stethoscope all over me, and it made me shiver. "That's a good girl," he kept telling me.

Next time I woke up, Joey was standing near the bed, looking at me. He was in his pajamas and Grandma was asleep on the bed next to me. It must have been very early in the morning or very late at night.

"Are you alive?" Joey asked.

"Of course I'm alive," I told him. My voice was so dry and hoarse it didn't sound like me. My throat and my ears hurt very bad, but Joey smiled at the sound of my voice and I smiled back.

"I'm glad you're not dead," Joey said. "They wouldn't let me come near you. Grandma's real mean. And Mom cries all the time. She thinks you're going to die."

"She does?" It was an intriguing thought.

"Yes—and so does Bobby. He snuck in yesterday, and he said he thought you were dead already. You were lying there so quiet, and you looked so horrible. . . ."

"Joey!"

Grandma was sitting straight up in bed.

Joey went flying out of the room.

"What was he telling you?" Grandma demanded.

"He says I'm going to die. Grandma, am I going to die?"

Grandma grabbed me and hugged me hard and rocked me and said, "Wait until I get my hands on him. I'll break his neck. I'll kill him."

I knew Grandma wouldn't let me die, and I fell asleep in her arms, sniffing the dry, old smell of her nightgown. The next day I could get up, and Grandma helped me walk to the bathroom. When I looked in the mirror, I saw a face that didn't look anything like mine. It was a red monster face with white pocks and puffy eyes and swollen lips. "God," I said, "I never saw anybody as ugly as me."

"It'll take a few days," Grandma said, "and you'll be back to normal."

I loved looking at my face in the mirror. I wanted to look at it from every angle. Grandma told me to stay in bed, and she gave me her old ivory hand mirror to look at myself. I slept a lot that day, and in between sleeping I looked at myself in the mirror. I felt very comfortable in bed, very happy to be there, and I hoped the hideous face in the mirror would not fade back to normal too fast.

Around five that evening, I woke up and saw

Grandma sitting in the living room with her feet up, sipping a beer. That's how I knew it was five. I could see her through the open french doors. She looked old and tired, and suddenly I felt sad thinking about Grandma being so old and tired. I wanted to do something to change it, but I couldn't think what. So I lay there looking at her, and feeling sadder and sadder. She must have felt my eyes on her because she turned her head and looked right at me. I didn't want her to know I'd been looking at her so I turned my eyes away.

"Grandma," I said, "I wasn't looking at you."

"That's all right," she said. "I don't mind if you do."

"Grandma!"

"What?"

"Grandma!"

"What?"

"When I'm better, Grandma, I'm going to do something for you. I don't know what, but something nice."

"Pat," Grandma said, "just get better fast, and that'll be the nicest thing you can do for me."

The next day, Lolly came over to see me. She brought me her two new puzzles, a box of crayons, a Queen Elizabeth I coloring book, and two paperback books by Lloyd Alexander.

"The books are from my mother. The rest's from me."

I said to say thank you to her mother, even though I had read all the Lloyd Alexander books in the fourth grade.

"You look awful. I didn't look as bad as you. Everybody says you had the worst case of anybody. My mother thought you might get encephalitis."

"What's that?"

"Some kind of brain fever."

"No kidding?"

"I'm going back to school tomorrow."

"I think I'll have to stay out for the whole week."

"But I can come and play with you. I'm going to skip Girl Scouts and my art class this week, but I have to go to ballet. So I can come all the other days and be with you."

On Friday, Bobby woke up with a fever, and Grandma turned mean again. Ever since I was first sick, Grandma had been talking real sweet and making me things I liked to eat, like chocolate pudding and mashed potatoes. But when Bobby came down sick, she resumed complaining and muttering under her breath and snapping at me.

I was feeling better by then and was pretty much out of bed even though my face was covered with scabs. I got Bobby set up on the couch in front of the TV, and the two of us tried to be inconspicuous.

After school, Lolly came to visit, and for the first time ever, Mrs. Scheiner came upstairs with her. I turned the TV off in the living room, and got Bobby to go lie down in his bedroom. The place was pretty messy, I guess, and Grandma was wearing her old, bright green sweater with the coffee stains down the front and her floppy slippers on her feet.

"I'm only staying for a minute," said Mrs. Scheiner, looking even more embarrassed than Grandma. "I wanted to help Lolly carry everything and I wanted to say hello to poor, old Pat. Well now, you really had quite a case—but I can see you're coming along very nicely. . . ." Mrs. Scheiner chattered away in her nervous, high-pitched voice. She was a small, thin, bright-eyed woman, dressed very stylishly in muted shades of tan and gray. Grandma stood over her, tall and large and very bright.

"Why don't you sit down, Mrs. Scheiner, and have a cup of tea?" Grandma said in a cranky voice.

"Oh no, thanks a million, but I couldn't. I've got to pick Greg up at the museum in fifteen minutes, and then I have to get over to the vet with our cat. She's been having trouble with one of her eyes, and . . ."

"It'll only take a few minutes," Grandma said grumpily.

"Oh, that's so nice of you, but I really must run. Thanks very much, and take care of *yourself*, Mrs. Hartman. I know it's no picnic being home with sick children. Good-bye, Pat, hurry up and get better. Be home by four-thirty, Lolly. Bye-bye."

It was Valentine's Day, and Mrs. Scheiner had brought a box of Valentine's Day cupcakes—pink-and-white ones with red hearts on top.

"Isn't that nice," Grandma muttered and banged off to the kitchen.

"And I brought you a bunch of Valentine's Day cards from the kids in the class. Look at this funny one from Jimmy Herndon. It says 'Guess Who?' but it's from him. He gave the same one to everybody. And here, this one's from Karen, and this one's from Diane."

Lolly had brought hers along, too, and we compared hers and mine. She had five cards and I had twenty-six.

"I guess you must be the most popular kid in the class," Lolly said.

"No, I'm not," I told her. "Joany Sussman is."

"No, she's not. You are."

"No, I'm not."

"Everybody likes you. Everybody wants to be your friend."

I felt bad that Lolly only had five valentines. "You know you would have had six," I told her, "but I was sick and didn't buy any."

"That's all right," Lolly said. "I know you're my best friend even though you didn't send me a valentine. But look, I made one for you."

She pulled out a homemade red construction paper envelope, with pink lipstick marks all over the outside. Inside was a big, round, white face covered with red heart-shaped chicken poxes. The face under the red spots had black hair and black eyes so I knew it was supposed to be me. In dark pink letters it said:

> Even though you are no beauty
> I feel it is my solemn duty

When I opened it up all the heart-shaped spots had disappeared from my face and were gathered together in a beautiful halo above my clear, sparkling face.

> To say you are my VALENTINE
> (And my best friend forever and ever)
> With lots of love and XXXXXs
> Lolly

"It's beautiful," I said, "but now I want to make one for you."

"Okay," said Lolly, "but I better help you because you're really a mess when it comes to art."

We sat at the kitchen table and cut up some of the other cards and then pasted them together on a piece of cardboard. Lolly did most of the pasting while I wrote a poem for her. I wrote:

> Lolly is sweet
> She can't be beat
> Our friendship's neat
> It's always a treat
> When we meet
> And eat
> Valentine's Day cupcakes
> (To my best friend forever and ever,
> Lolly Scheiner, from her best friend)
> Patricia Maddox

We each had two cupcakes, Bobby had one, and Joey had two when he came back from playing. Grandma refused to have any, and after Lolly left she said she thought Mrs. Scheiner had a lot of nerve coming over without calling first.

"She only came up to help Lolly carry the cupcakes and the cards and my homework."

"She's stuck-up," Grandma said. "Did you see how she wouldn't even sit down and have a cup of tea with me?"

"But Grandma, you didn't really want her to stay. You didn't *really* ask her very nicely."

"Don't you go telling me what I wanted or didn't want," Grandma yelled and gave me a little slap on my arm.

I knew I was better then. The next day, I went outside, and on Monday I returned to school. We took our class pictures later that week, and there are still a few scabs on my forehead and on one side of my chin. But I am standing next to Lolly and grinning. I was happy to be back in school and happy to be standing next to

Lolly. I didn't notice it then, but now when I look at the picture, I am struck for the first time at how clear and bright Lolly's face is. Maybe because mine is pocked with scabs, but Lolly's skin seems particularly smooth and radiant. She is wearing a blue plaid shirt, and her blue eyes are large and brilliant. There is still a lot of fat on her cheeks and on the stumpy fingers folded in her lap, and her braces gleam through her careful little smile. I couldn't know then what the future would hold for her, but now I can look back and see the first signs.

Chapter 7

Some of the girls in my sixth-grade class picture look like grown-ups. Heidi Jackson is standing next to Mrs. Morgan, and she is taller and bustier. She is also wearing gold earrings, a pink pantsuit, and has her hair flipped over one eye like a model. It's funny comparing her to Danny Friedman, who is standing next to her. He comes up to her ear and looks about half her age. Most of the boys look younger than the girls in the picture.

My hair is short and in my eyes. After sixth grade, I never let it grow long again. It's a new me in the sixth grade. I look older, my face is narrow, and my cheekbones seem pointy. I am not pretty—but I like my face. It is full of interesting ins and outs. Lolly is sitting in the front row while I am standing in the back row. You can see how Lolly's blonde hair is beginning to grow long. She never wore it short after sixth grade. Her face is more heart-shaped now, and you can see a funny little dimple in her left cheek.

By the time of the class picnic, Lolly's hair had grown to her shoulders, and she was wearing hair bands all the time. The class picnic was going to be held a week before our graduation from elementary school. Everybody in the class was supposed to bring something, and Mrs. Morgan asked us to let her know beforehand. Usually Grandma did not take kindly to potluck picnics or parties where the families of the involved students were expected to contribute.

I always preferred asking Mom when she was home. But Mom was seldom home or was sleeping when she was. So generally I had to deal with Grandma. I always expected some pretty heavy negotiations, usually ending with my bringing either the napkins or the paper cups. I seldom won out in any confrontation with my grandmother involving contributions. So this time, I was completely caught off guard.

"Sure," said Grandma, "you can bring the dessert."

"The dessert?" I stammered.

"Why not?" Grandma smiled. "It's a special occasion."

Terrified that she might consider baking a cake, I asked warily, "What kind of dessert?"

"Well, what about doughnuts? How many kids in the class?"

"Twenty-eight, and Mrs. Morgan."

"How about sixty doughnuts?"

"SIXTY DOUGHNUTS?"

"I'll ask Mr. Nagel. He won't mind."

Mr. Nagel was a friend of my grandmother's. He and Mrs. Nagel used to be her friends, but now that Mrs. Nagel had died nearly a year ago, only Mr. Nagel was left. He was a baker—for Doughnut Land—a small, thin, nervous-looking man, a little shorter and a lot thinner than my grandmother.

The night before the picnic, Mr. Nagel came over, carrying an enormous white box. Inside lay vast quantities of rainbow-colored doughnuts.

"What do you say to Mr. Nagel?" Grandma asked.

She was wearing her navy blue jacket dress and her pearls. She had makeup on, too—lipstick and powder that lay trapped inside the wrinkles on her neck.

"Thank you, Mr. Nagel," I chanted.

He laughed and nodded at me. "It's a pleasure," he said, and then laughed and nodded at Grandma. She laughed and nodded back at him, as if he'd just said something very clever.

Joey and Bobby came in and inspected the doughnuts.

"There's enough for you boys too," said Mr. Nagel. "I brought extra so you could enjoy yourselves tonight."

"What do you say to Mr. Nagel?" my grandmother coached.

"Thank you, Mr. Nagel," said the boys.

Then all three of us stood there, grinning at him and waiting for him to leave.

"Are you ready?" Mr. Nagel asked my grandmother.

"Just a sec," she said, flashing a big smile at him. She'd had a couple of new teeth put in a month or so ago and could smile now with her whole mouth open.

I told Lolly about it the next day at the picnic. I couldn't wait to tell her. "My grandmother went out to dinner last night with a man."

"Your grandmother!"

"My grandmother. They went to a Chinese restaurant, and then they went to the movies."

"I can't believe it."

"And she dressed up and put on makeup and acted silly. I don't know what's the matter with her."

"Maybe she's in love," Lolly said doubtfully.

"My grandmother with Mr. Nagel? He's a silly, little man with a skinny neck. Why would she be in love with Mr. Nagel?"

"I don't know," said Lolly, "but it certainly doesn't sound at all like your grandmother."

It bothered me a lot, almost as much as it bothered Mom. But today was the class picnic and I had brought sixty beautiful doughnuts. I couldn't help enjoying myself.

The picnic was held outside in Golden Gate Park. Some of the parents came along and helped Mrs. Morgan move tables together and set out the food. There were hot dogs, sandwiches, Jell-O–mold salads, pickles, potato chips, carrots, celery sticks, punch, cookies, and my doughnuts.

We played softball. I pitched for my team and we won. We had sack races, peanut races, and three-legged races. Lolly and I were partners, so naturally we came in last. But I didn't mind. I was captain of the Reds and Richie Kronberg of the Blues for Red Rover. My team won easily, and we all got red- and blue-striped balloons as prizes.

Nobody wanted to go home when three o'clock rolled around, so Mrs. Morgan laughed and said we could stay longer—she was in no hurry for the day to end. I heard her tell some of the mothers that this class had been a particularly lovable one. That she had enjoyed the children in this class—all the children—more than any other class she'd ever had. She even had tears in her eyes when she said it.

"She always does that," I heard Mrs. Kronberg say to Mrs. Scheiner in a low voice.

Mrs. Morgan was probably the most popular teacher in the school. She had no children of her own which was why, my grandmother said, she liked kids so much. I liked Mrs. Morgan. Next to Mr. Evans, I liked her the best in elementary school. I'm not sure how much we learned in sixth grade but nobody was ever unhappy in Mrs. Morgan's class.

Mr. Evans was married now—to Meg. She was going to law school at Hastings, he told me, and was planning to go into civil-rights law.

"What does that mean?"

"That she wants to help people who are minorities or women or poor or old—she wants them to have the same rights as everybody else."

"Well, how can they have the same rights as everybody else if they're different?" I asked him.

I had come to say good-bye to Mr. Evans and ask him to sign my autograph album. Tomorrow was graduation, and then I was all through with elementary school. He wrote *To Pat Maddox, my ugly duckling, who just might become a swan if she keeps her head above water. All best wishes, Jason Evans.*

"Do me a favor, Pat."

"What?"

"Don't become a lawyer."

"You can be sure of that," I told him. "I want to be a doctor."

"How come?"

I couldn't tell him it was because of the kitchen in Lolly Scheiner's house. I couldn't say that every time I went into that kitchen, stood inside the gleaming rays from the stainless-steel sink, and watched the lights on the automatic stove flash on and off—I thought to myself how rich doctors must be and how vastly more desirable it was to be inside the Scheiner's gleaming, all-electric kitchen than inside the one in my home. I liked to think that when I became a doctor, I would have a kitchen like the Scheiners' and that my grandma would be happy. It was a problem, though, imagining my grandmother surrounded by such a kitchen. In her old green sweater, floppy slippers, and messy hair, she didn't seem to belong in my daydream.

"I want to help people," I said weakly to Mr. Evans. He looked at me suspiciously.

"And I'm good at math and science," I said quickly.

He nodded. "Yes, you are. You've got a good head," he said. "Use it. Don't sell yourself short." He gave me a little tap on my head, and shoved me out of his room.

"Good-bye, Mr. Evans," I screeched. "Don't worry, I'll come back and see you."

"That's what I'm worrying," he said.

Lolly and I sat together the next day for the graduation ceremony. Mom said she was going to come, and I kept looking over my shoulder for her. I had a new dress, a white one with pink roses over the front, and two pink barrettes in my hair. My breasts were beginning to grow, but the rest of me was still narrow and bony. Those new breasts felt like they belonged to somebody else, but Lolly said I'd get used to them. Even though she was shorter than me, her breasts were larger. She was already wearing a bra, and her period had begun three months ago. I was jealous that something was happening to her before it happened to me. But I didn't say so. I always had trouble admitting things like that to Lolly.

"There's my mother and my father too," Lolly whispered. "He didn't know if he could come."

The kids in the band were beginning to tune up their instruments, but still there was no sight of my mother. I stood up and craned my neck toward the back.

Lolly reached over and took my hand. "Listen, Pat," she said, "my parents are taking me out to lunch. They said you could come too."

"My mother's taking me to lunch," I told her and then wondered why I said it. Mr. Cardoza, the bandleader, was motioning for all his musicians to get ready, but my mother still hadn't come.

"But if she . . . if she . . . doesn't make it . . ."

"Oh, I'm meeting her later then," I said angrily, pulling my hand away from Lolly's.

"Pat . . ." she whispered and she took my hand again. She understood. She knew I wasn't angry at her. She knew I felt bad. She knew how my mother was always disappointing me even though I never said so. I never had to say so to Lolly. She was my best friend.

There was a big, painful lump in my throat as I watched Mr. Cardoza lift his baton and we prepared to rise and sing "The Star Spangled Banner."

"Oh, there she is, Pat. There she is," Lolly said, squeezing my hand.

My mother had just come through the back door. Grandma was with her and so was Mr. Nagel. Three people had come to my graduation. Three people!

Lolly pressed my hand hard, and we continued holding hands as we rose and began to sing.

My mother looked pretty on the day I graduated. She had a new frosted hairdo, teased up high, and a pale blue dress and matching sweater. But my grandmother was wearing a red-and-white pantsuit and had mascara on her eyelashes. She was wearing straw-colored sandals and carried a matching shoulder-strap purse. Mr. Nagel was standing very close to her, holding her just under her elbow, when I joined them after the ceremony.

I couldn't take my eyes off my grandmother. If she were somebody else's grandmother, I wouldn't have noticed her at all. But my grandmother had no business looking like that.

"Lolly's parents are taking her out to lunch," I mumbled finally, looking down at my grandmother's shoes. "They want me to come too."

"I should say not," said my grandmother's voice from above. "You're coming with us."

"We're going to have our own private party," came Mr. Nagel's voice. "This is an occasion, after all."

I could hear the two of them laughing. Not my mother. I couldn't hear her laughing. "I should go to work," I heard her say in a sulky voice. "I'm late as it is."

"That's all right," my grandmother said in a phony, bright, tinkly voice. "You can come in late today. Mr. Nagel would be insulted if you didn't come."

"That's right," said Mr. Nagel. "I'd be insulted."

"We're going out to lunch," I told Lolly, "so I can't come with you." I made a face, but I really wasn't upset. Even though I wished my grandmother didn't

69

look the way she looked, and even though I wished that Mr. Nagel had stayed in the doughnut store, it was my graduation day and it wasn't very often that I was taken out to lunch.

Lolly and I hugged each other, and she whispered for me to come over to her house early the next morning. She and her mother were going shopping for clothes she would need over the summer, and I could come along with them. Her whole family was going away for six weeks to Europe. Lolly and I tried not to think of being apart for six weeks. We had another week and a half before she was to go, and we planned to spend all our free time together.

Mr. Nagel owned a shiny blue Dodge. It was very neat and clean inside. He helped my grandmother into the front seat and held the back door open for my mother and me. She looked out the window while we drove across the Golden Gate Bridge into Sausalito and never said one word during the trip. My grandmother bubbled along to Mr. Nagel and to me and acted as if she'd spent all her life driving around in shiny blue cars, dressed in tight, red-and-white pantsuits.

We had lunch in a restaurant overlooking the bay, and Mr. Nagel said I could order anything I wanted. I studied the menu over and over again until my mother said crankily that she didn't want to spend all day waiting for me to make up my mind. So I ordered a cheeseburger, french fries, and a strawberry milk shake.

My grandmother and mother had Bloody Marys, and avocados stuffed with shrimp. Mr. Nagel had the avocado stuffed with shrimp but no Bloody Mary. He said he had stomach troubles and couldn't drink anymore. He laughed a lot and so did my grandmother. When he gave me a ten-dollar bill for a graduation present, I decided he wasn't such a terrible person after all. I even let him sign my autograph album. He wrote: *Best Wishes for a wonderful future to a very charming young lady. From William Nagel, a good friend of the family.*

Chapter 8

If it hadn't been for Joey's balloon that day in the zoo, I guess seventh grade would have been one complete bust. To start with, something was different about Lolly. I didn't know what it was at first, and maybe it wasn't until we got our class pictures that I finally figured it out. But something was different about Lolly and whatever it was, I didn't like it.

I never was one to take kindly to change. Even now, when I have only exciting times to look forward to, I don't want to go on. I want to stop right here, hold on to the edges of my present with all my fingernails, dig them in deep, and keep my life from changing. I want to, but I won't.

Until I was nearly twelve, nothing changed about my grandmother. She was always there—a thick-ankled, sharp-tongued, frowsy, beer-guzzling old lady who loved me best. That's the way I liked it. That's the way

I wanted it to continue. But the more Mr. Nagel came around, the more my grandmother changed.

She had her teeth fixed. That was the beginning of the end. She had her hair cut with curly wisps showing across her forehead. She stopped shuffling around in slippers and started powdering her wrinkles, lipsticking her old mouth, and putting mascara on her eyelashes. She bought new clothes—bright ones, revealing ones.

"How about acting your age?" my mother snapped at her one night after she had displayed her latest purchase, a pink pantsuit with a slinky, low-cut, lavender blouse.

"That's what I'm doing," giggled my grandmother. "I'm not really an old lady yet, and I'm tired of acting like one."

My mother said a lot that night and used words like *disgusting* and *laughingstock* and *ashamed* over and over again. But nothing she said made a dent. My grandmother didn't even grow angry. She just kept saying it was time for her to enjoy life, and that's exactly what she was doing.

They took us to the zoo on that cold, blowy day in January. I don't remember where my mother was. Maybe she was working. Maybe she was sleeping. Maybe she was out with her friends. But that year my mother and I were closer than we had ever been before and ever would be afterward. We had a common cause—my grandmother. It was a silent treaty—we never spoke openly to each other—but we were allies.

My mother attacked frontally. Every new outfit my grandmother bought set my mother off. She took the offensive. I fought a rear-guard action, a quiet, sneaky but effective one. I sulked. I mooned around the house. I displayed my disapproval in quiet sullenness. In the face of my grandmother's happy, lively chatter, I grew more and more silent. Sometimes I could see her watching me thoughtfully, unhappily, I hoped.

It was Mr. Nagel's idea to take us to the zoo. He had no children of his own, no grandchildren, and he kept saying how much he loved children. Anything we said, he laughed foolishly. He was forever slipping us quarters, bringing us doughnuts, patting us anywhere he could reach. Joey, being the youngest, was his favorite.

Neither Bobby nor I wanted to go to the zoo, but Grandma insisted. She looked particularly horrible that day—in a pair of cheap, crinkly black boots, a black turtleneck shirt, an orange coat, and frosted orange lipstick to match.

Mr. Nagel never stopped buying all through that afternoon—hot dogs, french fries, Cokes, popcorn. . . . He bought us Cracker Jacks, candy bars, ice cream. Anything edible that was for sale, he bought us. He ran back and forth buying things for us and exuding a faint odor of grease.

He bought Joey a balloon. A huge, pink Mickey Mouse balloon that tugged at its bright green string. Joey was nine—too old for a balloon, and he looked unhappily over at Bobby and me. We were grinning at him. Mr. Nagel didn't understand. "You both want balloons too?" he asked. "I didn't know. I thought maybe you're too old, but if you want balloons . . ."

"No, no, thank you, Mr. Nagel," I said with cold superiority. "We are too old, but thank you anyway."

I looked over at my grandmother, hoping to share a superior smile with her, but she was watching Mr. Nagel, shaking her head at him. "Willie, Willie," she said, "stop it! You're too good. Stop it!"

They looked at each other and laughed. There was such happiness in their look and their laugh, such loving comfort in each other, that I wanted to die. For twelve years my grandmother had loved me the best in the world, but on that day in the zoo, I knew it was all over.

"Here, Baby Joey," I snapped. "Hold onto your balloon, but don't wet your pants."

Both Bobby and I piled on Joey—teasing him, prodding him, focusing all our frustrations on him. Mr. Nagel, outside of a few worried glances over at Joey, was too intent on my grandmother to feel any pain. And my grandmother, laughing like a teen-age girl, daintily nibbling away on the hot dogs, popcorn, french fries, and all the other "burnt offerings" Mr. Nagel presented her, ignored us. They held hands, and we tormented Joey. There were tears in his eyes but he held onto that pink Mickey Mouse balloon. Why he didn't let it go, I don't know. He even tied it around his wrist. It stood straight up, the green string taut under the bouncy, pink mouse head.

But when we got home, the balloon drooped, and lay on the ground. I kept trying, unsuccessfully, to make it float. And I wondered why.

I guess that was the real beginning for me. That was how I became me now. It was Joey's balloon and the misery I felt over my grandmother. It's funny how so much that's good about me comes from so many of the bad things that happened in my life. If Mrs. Scheiner hadn't opened her big mouth, maybe I never would have known how different I was from the rest of my family. If Grandma had never married Mr. Nagel and left me, maybe nothing would have changed. And if poor Joey hadn't been given a silly, pink Mickey Mouse balloon (along with shameful abuse from me) where would I be now?

All that weekend I sulked and snapped whenever my grandmother talked to me, but inside my anger, the question of the balloon remained unresolved.

It was helium that made it stay up.

He, Atomic number 2, Atomic weight 4.0026

Now I know something about helium. I know about elements and gases and mass and energy. I know that for every question there is an answer—and for every answer, another question. Nothing stops in this world, and I started with a spent balloon that would not rise because all the helium had dissipated.

Mrs. Barricini, my science teacher in the seventh grade, told me about the helium in the balloon. We talked for a long time on Monday afternoon—she talked, and I listened. After a while, she took the limp balloon that I had brought her, blew it up, and then released it. She laughed as it ricocheted wildly around the room. "That's the basis of rocketry," she told me. "Release gas under pressure and see what happens."

I guess I went crazy in the seventh grade. All I could think about was rocket engines. I took Bobby and Joey down to the park with me any afternoon I was free. They used to make those little toy model planes, and I put balloon engines on them.

I read everything I could find about rockets, and then I began reading about space. I made a little refracting telescope out of a couple of cardboard tubes and old magnifying-glass lenses. I tried to look at the moon through it from out of my bedroom window and was disappointed at its fuzzy whiteness. I wanted to see the rings of Saturn, explore Andromeda, and peer into the dark holes of space. I found myself increasingly impatient and frustrated.

One Sunday, I met Mr. Evans down in the park with his baby son, Luke. The baby was creeping all over the grass, putting everything into his mouth, and yowling whenever Mr. Evans tried to stop him. It was hard for him to focus his full attention on me, but you could see he was impressed when he held my latest six-balloon jet rocket in his hand.

"You did this yourself?"

"Uh-huh, but it's only balloons. It's against the law to blast off any real rocket engines. Besides, I'm getting bored with it. I'd like to make a reflecting telescope, but I don't have the right tools."

Luke was putting a large wad of chewing gum into his mouth, and Mr. Evans had to grab it away before it disappeared. Luke's cheeks turned almost as red as his hair, and he screamed his head off and beat at his father's chest when Mr. Evans picked him up.

"Listen, Pat, you can come over and work in my shop any time," he said breathlessly. "I'm on Fourth and Anza. We've got a house now and a basement full of tools."

I started work on a reflecting telescope. Mr. Evans helped me assemble my materials and work out the mathematics. He took me to the planetarium and to a few meetings of the Sidewalk Astronomers where I could see the skies through real telescopes.

I began showing up at his house most Sunday mornings. The shop was always available to me. Often he'd be working on some repair for his house. We'd work along together, and often he'd stop what he was doing to come watch me or even join in. New tools suddenly appeared. The lighting over his worktable improved.

He said he needed it, but I knew it was because of me.

Mrs. Evans told me to call her Meg, but I couldn't do it. She was in her last year of law school and looked as if she never had time to comb her hair or sew up the ripped seams in her peasant blouses.

Sometimes, in between studying, she'd come downstairs and watch us work or join in our conversations. She and Mr. Evans liked to be together. They smiled at each other a lot and were forever touching each other's hands or leaning on each other's shoulders. I didn't feel left out with them the way I did with my grandmother and Mr. Nagel. It made me happy to be there, and I hated it when they fought. One Sunday, Mrs. Evans went banging out of the house after calling Mr. Evans some pretty horrendous names. It frightened me and I ran home, crying and worrying that everything was going to change.

But next Sunday, everything was the same. I began sitting for them. At first for only a couple of hours when Luke was asleep; but in the spring, they let me do it sometimes when he was awake.

Grandma and Mr. Nagel were married in May. My mother never stopped arguing up until the end. She called my grandmother "selfish" and "ridiculous." She said Mr. Nagel was a "moron" and that he would never be welcome in her house if Grandma married him. She said that Grandma was abandoning us and that she, my mother, was sure to have a nervous breakdown.

My grandmother never lost her temper. She said she wasn't going to the moon, only to Daly City, and that we could visit her whenever we wanted, and of course, she'd come to see us too. But once, a few days before her wedding, she did say to my mother in a tight, very controlled voice that it was time for my mother to grow up and think of other people besides herself.

She talked to me too, one night, when my mother was working and the boys were watching TV.

"You're the one," she told me, "who's going to get the worst of it. But stand up for yourself. Don't let her push you around."

"Mom never pushes me around," I told her.

"She will once I'm gone. She'll try to get you to carry the load, but don't do it."

She reached out, took my hand and shook it as if to pump her thoughts into me. I looked at her face, covered with powder and paint, at her hair under the new frosted rinse she was using, and saw—my grandmother. She was my grandmother and I couldn't bear to lose her. In a second I was in her lap, big twelve-year-old me, my face buried in her shoulder, bawling, "Don't go, Grandma, don't do it!"

She patted my back, kissed my head, and said maybe I should come live with her. But I didn't want to live with her and Mr. Nagel. Only her. I raised my teary, bleary face to hers and saw she was shaken. "Don't go, Grandma," I sobbed, "I love you so much."

"I love you too, Pat," she said, "but you're growing up, and in a few years you'll be off and running. You're not going to need me anymore. But I love you, darling, you know that. I love you and I love Mr. Nagel too."

"Mr. Nagel!"

"Yes, Mr. Nagel," she said, stiffening. "It's the first time in my life somebody wants to do for me instead of the other way around. Your grandpa was a good man, may he rest in peace. I'm not saying anything about your grandpa, Pat. He was a good man, a handsome man, too, and big and strong. He did the best he could, I know that, but everything he touched went wrong. I worked and worked and worked while he was alive, and after he died there was your mother, and then there were the three of you to take care of. Now Willie—Mr. Nagel—he wants to take care of *me*. He's got a little money, a house—he's going to retire soon. He wants to travel, have a good time. He likes to laugh, and I like to laugh too. I forgot how much I like to laugh and have a good time. I used to, when I was a girl, and now I have a chance again, Pat."

I lay back against her shoulder, thinking I should tell her, *Go ahead, Grandma, have a good time. Don't think about us.* But I couldn't say it. I just lay there and said nothing.

I went to her wedding, though, with Joey and Bobby. We chipped in and bought her a tea set in Chinatown. Mom refused to go to the wedding and didn't give a present. She told us not to go either, but we did. I wore my white-and-pink graduation dress from sixth grade, which was so tight now across the chest, I could hardly breathe. The boys looked handsome—especially Joey.

Grandma wore a blue lace dress, a large blue hat, and matching shoes. She looked like an old lady trying to look young. I thought she looked awful, but Mr. Nagel kept saying she looked like an angel. We went with them to City Hall, and then afterward, he drove us back to his house in Daly City. Some of his friends and neighbors put a big sign up outside his door, BEST WISHES MR. AND MRS. WILLIAM NAGEL, and threw rice at them when they got out of the car. Little Mr. Nagel even carried my big grandmother over the threshold, struggling manfully under his giggling burden.

There were bridge tables set out in the living room covered with food and bottles of champagne. The house looked so clean and shiny, so full of well-kept furniture and thick carpets that I couldn't see my grandmother ever finding a comfortable spot.

It didn't hit me for a few weeks that Grandma really was gone. She talked to us over the phone and she came to see us. Sometimes we went there and even slept over. But at night, Mom and I shared the big bed in the bedroom, and after school, when I came home, Grandma wasn't shuffling around anymore in her slippers and old green sweater.

It wasn't too bad at first until the novelty wore off. My mother even tried to run things herself. I guess we all knew she couldn't, but there was an excitement in the beginning, pretending she might.

With all the changes in my life, I didn't really get around to thinking about Lolly until it was nearly summer. Class pictures came late in the seventh grade, and it was then, looking at Lolly's face in the picture, that I suddenly realized what it was that had been different about Lolly all that year and what it was that I hadn't figured out until just then.

Lolly had become a beauty.

Chapter 9

She was probably the last one to realize it. She had been a little fat girl for so long that she went right on thinking of herself that way even after she slimmed down and became a beauty.

Not that she was ever very slim. There are no corners or angles on Lolly—no sharp edges, the way there are on me. When you look at my face, you know exactly where my bones are underneath the skin. When you look at Lolly's face, you forget all about bones. The colors are strong in Lolly's face—deep blue eyes, bright blonde hair, pink cheeks and lips, and a wonderfully delicate, smooth blue white skin. She was fat for so long that she still looks at you in a wary, apprehensive way. I've seen the same look on the faces of other fat people. It says, I know you think I'm gross, but I don't know if you're going to make fun of me.

Lolly always had more clothes than anybody else,

and she may have thought at one time that she would become a fashion designer. But I could have told her that's not where her talents lay. Maybe I didn't know where they did lie, or maybe even if she had any talents at all. Shame on me. Now I know that I sold her short, just as her family did. But that is the problem with beauty. If you have it, nobody sees beyond it.

Lolly always drew well, but she had no taste at all when it came to clothes. I always thought it was her mother's fault. Mrs. Scheiner loved buying clothes for Lolly, loved dressing her in all the current styles. Lolly always had more sets of things, more neat, tidy, expensive, fashionable outfits than anybody else. She dressed the way people think they want to dress if they only had the money, but seldom do unless they have no imagination at all. With all her clothes, Lolly's wardrobe was boring.

But in eighth grade, nobody wants to stand out. Of course, with Lolly's lovely face, she couldn't help standing out. If she had coupled her beauty with a flair for clothes, the girls might have hated her. But they didn't hate her. They were jealous of her, but more and more they flocked to her for security.

In eighth grade, there was a regrouping and a reshuffling.

Ever since fifth grade, Lolly had stopped being the butt. Nobody picked on her for a few years, but nobody sought her out either. She moved in that misty middle ground between approval and disapproval. In the eighth grade, she arrived.

You spend a lot of time in junior high working out who you are. I thought, at first, it was going to be easy for me. Thanks to Joey's balloon, I had become a scientist. I told myself that over and over again as I watched new colonies of pimples sprouting on my forehead every morning in the mirror. I wasn't just an ordinary boy-crazy girl who *had* to worry about her appearance. I was me, Patricia Maddox, another Madame Curie, a new star in the scientific universe. Sometimes though, I forgot, late at night, when I prayed desperately to God for a smooth, clear complexion.

Just before my thirteenth birthday, my period finally arrived. With it came the new fashioning of my old body—bigger breasts, hair, sweat, and more pimples. My clothes didn't fit. I needed to wear a bra. I smelled like somebody else, and there was a crawling, creeping under my skin that plagued me continually. I hurt. My heart beat faster. I went up and I came down. I cried and I looked at boys in a different way.

But in spite of all the changes, I knew who I was. Other girls still had to work it out for themselves, and many of them were afraid. Many of them turned to Lolly. They needed a sure thing. Anyone as beautiful as Lolly, they figured, was bound to make it.

First it was the girls, then the boys. I didn't mind— until later. Everybody always liked me—the girls, I mean, and the boys too. Kenny Saxton and I still hung around together sometimes at his house on rainy afternoons.

"Are you going to Diane Frost's party this Saturday night?" he asked me one day. He was catching up to me in height—both of us were just about the same size now. He had grown very skinny, and a large, knobby Adam's apple bobbled up and down in the middle of his throat. Kenny was smart too. He had become interested in paleotaxonomy, particularly extinct marine invertebrate animals. There was a lab over at the science museum where Kenny worked one or two afternoons a week. Nobody liked listening to him talk about extinct marine invertebrate animals. I let him talk to me, though, and I listened as long as he let me talk about telescopes and space and he listened.

"I don't know. Are you?"

Kenny made a face. "My mother says I should go but I don't know. Are you going?"

"I don't know. Are you?"

"I asked you first."

"I don't know. If Lolly goes, maybe I'll go."

"Lolly's going."

"How do you know?"

"She told me."

I was hurt. "She didn't tell me. I didn't even know she was invited. Diane Frost never even liked Lolly very much."

"Anyway," Kenny said, "If you go, can I go with you?"

"Well, sure, but you live right across the street from Diane."

"But I don't want to go by myself. You could pick me up on your way over."

I asked Lolly why she didn't tell me she'd been invited to Diane Frost's party. "I didn't know if you'd been invited," she said.

"Me?" I was outraged. "I'm always invited to her parties," I told her.

"Well, I just didn't know. And I wasn't going to go if she didn't invite you."

Something occurred to me. "When did she invite you?" I asked.

"Last Tuesday, Wednesday . . . I can't remember exactly."

"She just invited me yesterday."

"Good," said Lolly. "Then I'm definitely going."

"Wait a minute!" Some of the pieces were beginning to fit. "You mean she wasn't going to invite *me*?"

"Well," Lolly said anxiously, "it's just that it was going to be a girl-boy party."

"So?"

"Well, she had more girls than she needed."

"So why did she invite you?"

"I guess because she knew I could bring along four or five boys. But I told her I wouldn't come if you weren't invited."

"But that's crazy," I protested. "I could bring some boys too . . . Kenny Saxton, for instance. I'm bringing Kenny Saxton. He wasn't going to come without me."

"Oh, Kenny Saxton!" said Lolly.

Thanks to Lolly, we ended up with nine boys and seven girls at the party. Of the nine boys, six of them circled Lolly the whole evening. Of the three remaining, one (Kenny Saxton) ate potato chips, one took care of the records and record player, and the third kept his arm on Karen Stein's shoulder the whole evening.

Lolly wore a pair of pink jeans with a blue-and-pink flowered T-shirt and a pink cardigan. She seemed lit up with a pink light inside all those pink clothes. She radiated pink.

The miserable clump of five scorned girls radiated jealousy.

"Look at the way she's sticking out her bust," Rachel Harris whispered to the others. "That's why all the boys are interested in her."

"Bull," I said loyally. "It's because she's such a nice girl, and so beautiful."

"I think she's stuck-up," Helen Young said. "Just

because she's rich and her mother buys her all those classy clothes. . . ."

"You're just jealous," I told her.

But I was suffering too. One of the boys crouched around Lolly was Ronny Cabell. I had first noticed him in seventh grade, but he still hadn't noticed me. My feelings for Ronny Cabell were so deep and so powerful I hadn't even told Lolly about them. Now, as I watched him gyrate in front of her, and saw her radiating her pink light in his direction, I was happy I hadn't.

Kenny Saxton returned from his post near the potato chips. "You want to go home?" he asked me.

The girls regarded me now with respect. Maybe it was only Kenny Saxton, but even so, he was a boy.

"Okay," I said, swelling slightly with pride. After all, I had come to the party with a boy and I was leaving with a boy. It didn't compare to Lolly's conquest of Ronny Cabell and the five other boys, or even to that arm around Karen Stein's shoulder, but it was better than nothing.

"My mother said she'll run you home," Kenny told me, yawning. "That was really boring."

It was still early, so we played chess at his house, ate some ginger cookies and ice cream with his parents, and Mrs. Saxton drove me home.

"Wasn't the party fun?" Lolly asked over the phone the next morning.

"It was fun for you," I told her. "All the boys were interested in you."

"Were they?" she asked softly. "I didn't notice."

"Lolly," I told her, "you're getting to be a killer."

She cleared her throat. "Listen Pat, they'd like you

too if you didn't just plunk yourself down in a corner and act bored."

"I never do."

"And then, you should have dressed up a little bit. You had that old, gray YMCA shirt on with your baggy corduroy pants. You could have worn . . ."

"Lolly, cut it out."

"And you have to know how to talk to boys. They're very shy at this age. . . ."

"I didn't know you were Dear Abby," I snapped. "And please don't give me any advice. I don't need it, and I don't want it. I know perfectly well how to talk to boys. They've always managed to understand me when I speak to them. So please, just mind your own business."

"Okay Pat, don't be angry," Lolly said meekly.

But there was a reshuffling in our friendship too. After all those years of looking after Lolly and protecting her, suddenly she didn't need my protection anymore. Suddenly, it looked as if I might need hers. And I hated it.

She knew how to talk to boys—and men too. She certainly knew how to talk to Mr. O'Brien. He was the metal-shop teacher, and I wanted to take metal shop. I could handle myself pretty well by now, thanks to Mr. Evans, with a hammer and screwdriver, but I needed to learn how to weld. Mr. O'Brien didn't allow girls in his shop. Nowadays, no teacher could get away with such obvious sexism, but when I was in the eighth grade he could.

Girls were supposed to take homemaking classes in my junior high while the boys took shop. I didn't want homemaking. For one thing, my homemaking responsibilities, since my grandmother left, were coming out of my ears. But mainly, I needed to know how to handle metals for my work on telescope fittings.

Mr. O'Brien said no. No girls allowed. I spoke to my homeroom teacher, Mr. Henderson. He said it was fine with him *if* Mr. O'Brien agreed. Mr. O'Brien did not agree. He had too many boys interested in metal shop and boys needed it more than girls. I went to my counselor, Mrs. Barducci. She said it was fine with her *if* Mr. O'Brien agreed. Mr. O'Brien continued not to agree.

"Call the ACLU," Kenny Saxton advised.

"Go and see him one more time," Lolly said, "and I'll go with you."

We both waited for him one afternoon outside his shop. His face hardened when he saw me standing by the doorway.

"Well? What do *you* want?" he said.

"I'm going to the ACLU," I told him, "if you don't let me take shop. I'm going to write letters to the newspapers and maybe even picket the school."

"Ha!" replied Mr. O'Brien.

But then Lolly was speaking.

"What?" he asked, looking over at her.

"Please, Mr. O'Brien," she said in a very soft, very small voice, "please let my friend take metal shop." Her blue eyes opened very wide, and her cheeks glowed pinky pink. "She's a very smart girl, and very good in science. Everybody is really impressed with her. My father—he's a doctor, Mr. O'Brien, and he knows all about you. My brothers had you for shop."

"What's your last name, young lady?" Mr. O'Brien asked.

"Lorraine Scheiner, Mr. O'Brien. My brothers are Michael and Greg Scheiner. My father said they were all thumbs before you got them, and now they're both going to be doctors. Michael goes to Stanford and he made a beautiful silver inlaid box for my mother."

Mr. O'Brien grunted. "Nice boy—I remember him. And Greg too. Very nice boys." He looked at me. "Very nice manners."

"And my father thinks Pat might become a doctor too. She's very smart but she really needs your help. Please, Mr. O'Brien, couldn't you make an exception— just this once?"

"Why did you do that?" I yelled at her when we were outside.

Lolly's eyes opened in surprise. "I got you in, didn't I?"

"But not that way," I protested. "That way was disgusting."

Lolly shrugged. "You needed the class, right? What do you care how you got in? You're in."

"You made him feel he was Superman instead of a retard shop teacher. How could you demean yourself?"

"I didn't demean myself," Lolly said, looking troubled. "I did it for you."

It rankled inside me all that term. How I hated that man! But Lolly was right. If it wasn't for her, I never would have gotten into the metal shop that term. I hated Mr. O'Brien, but I learned how to weld. The next term he allowed two other girls to take his shop, and the following term it was open to everybody.

It wasn't my way. It wasn't my way then and it never will be my way. I would have fought him head on. I would have called in the ACLU, written to the papers, picketed the school. History was on my side. I would have won out—but not in time for me to take his class in the eighth grade, when I needed it the most.

In our class picture for the eighth grade, I am standing next to Lolly on one side, and Ronny Cabell is standing on the other. He is taller than she by about half a head and has a faint dark fuzz over his upper lip. He sent her a note which she didn't keep. But I memorized it when she showed it to me, and used to daydream that he sent it to me. The note said:

> Dear Lolly,
>   I am writing this with a pencil you dropped on your way past my desk in English. It is a little stump of a pencil, #2 "Supreme." That's the way I feel about you except I would change the number to #1. If you want the pencil back you will have to come bowling with me on Saturday afternoon. Even if you don't want the pencil back, why don't you come anyway?
>   Ronny

Ronny is one of the few tall boys in our class picture. The others are still pretty much shorter than the girls. Lolly has a very happy smile on her face, and her hair is down below her shoulders. I look smart. For the first time in any class picture, I am beginning to look like a scientist. I have a thoughtful line between my eyes and am biting down on my lower lip, deep in thought. Nobody would know from the intelligent look on my face that I wasn't thinking about $E = MC^2$. Nobody would know I was thinking about Ronny Cabell.

Chapter 10

Although I had suspected for some time, it was not until I was fourteen, in ninth grade, that my mother finally admitted she didn't know who my father was.

"You said his name was Eddie Rice," I told her.

"I never did," she yelled.

"Yes you did."

"No I didn't."

It was because of Joey that I finally found it out for sure. I'd kept at her ever since second grade, but she never let on until she exploded that night. Joey was eleven now, in Mrs. Morgan's sixth-grade class, and failing in math. And it was almost impossible to fail in anything in Mrs. Morgan's class.

"Mrs. Morgan said it's hard to believe Pat and I come from the same family," he announced one night at dinner.

"Well, Mrs. Morgan should keep her big mouth

shut," said my mother, fiddling around with her spaghetti. Bobby had cooked that night and, as usual, had dumped too much pepper in the spaghetti sauce.

"She said the same thing when I was in her class," Bobby said.

"I'll help you," I told Joey. "I told you before I'd help you, but you're just not interested. If you worked a little harder, you'd be able to do it. It's easy."

"It's easy for you," Joey said, "but I never understand any of it."

"Just let me work with you. You'll see . . ."

That's when he said it, and my mother hit the ceiling. "It's because you have a different father. That's why you're so smart."

My mother cut loose then. "Is that what she said, the bitch?" my mother shouted. "Well, there's plenty of smart people on my side of the family, let me tell you. Your Aunt Barbara's no slouch, and my Uncle Wallace is an engineer, and your father had a good head on his shoulders. If he'd lived, he was going to get a real estate license. Who does she think she is?"

"But Mom . . ." Joey tried in his slow, soft voice.

"She's got some nerve. And both of you are just as smart as Pat. She just works harder. If you did half as much as she does, you'd be way smarter than her."

"What are you picking on me for?" I yelled at her. "I didn't say anything."

"Maybe not," she shouted, "but you think you're so great. You go around here like you know everything and we're all dirt under your feet. Well, you don't have to go thinking you're so special. For all I know, your father could have been a psycho or a junky. If I knew who he was, I'd hand you over to him on a silver platter."

She knew she'd gone too far after she said it. She kept on blustering and pretending to be sore, but when Joey finally managed to say, "But Mom, it wasn't Mrs. Morgan who said it's because Pat had a different father. It was Bobby," my mother finally shut up and looked nervously at me.

Later, when we were alone, she said it happened after a dance. She'd had too much to drink, and there was a boy there who had a car and offered to take her home. She said she thought he was a college student, and she couldn't actually remember what he looked like. Daddy, the boys' father, had gone to high school with her, loved her very much, and wanted to marry her even though he knew she was pregnant. My mother also said she didn't mean what she'd said before, and that she was proud of me and loved me just as much as the boys.

She was always saying that she loved me the same as the boys, but I knew she didn't. Not that she really loved any of us very much. But I was certainly down on the bottom of the heap. My grandmother was right. After she left, my mother changed toward me. Before, it was as if all of us were kids and Grandma was the grown-up. With Grandma gone, I became the grown-up while Mom remained a kid along with the boys. She didn't want the responsibility of running a household, but she resented me for assuming it.

I guess I nagged her a lot, but somebody had to keep at her or nothing would ever be done. As it was, the three of us did most of the shopping, cleaning, laundry, and cooking. Often I had to shout, but the house looked even better than when Grandma was with us. And Bobby was turning into a fabulous cook. He liked pepper too much, but he could make barbecued chicken, spaghetti, meat loaf, and sweet-and-sour pork. He could make brownies, oatmeal cookies, and pineapple upside-down cake. He kept learning more and more recipes and after a while he did all the cooking while Joey and I cleaned and shopped. So all we expected from my mother was that she look after herself and give us some money.

Sometimes, when she talked on the telephone to one of her friends, you could hear her laugh a deep, happy belly laugh. But when she was with us, she never laughed like that. My mother didn't mind working, and she loved going off with her friends. When she was home, she mostly slept or talked on the telephone. The three of us knew, even if she didn't say so (which she did), that she would be a lot happier if she wasn't saddled with three kids. By the time I was fourteen, it didn't bother me so much anymore, and I tried not to expect too much from her. The boys didn't seem to mind either. When Grandma left, they figured I was there to look after them, and they were right.

What I did mind was letting go of the daydream I used to sink into whenever I needed it. He was there, my father, the old father, Eddie Rice, the one who married my mother. In my daydream, he returned one day to find me and take me away with him. Maybe he'd had amnesia or was engaged in a secret mission for the government. I could be vague in my own daydream about why he'd disappeared for fourteen years. But finally he came to find me. There was nothing vague about that, although the details of our joyful reunion could be adjusted to suit my different moods.

Now I had to let it go. How could I daydream about a predatory boy at a dance, who took advantage of a young, drunken girl, and be proud that he was my father? Other daydreams took its place. They tugged and pulled at the narrow margins of my life and brought me comfort. I suppose I'll always be a daydreamer. I'm not ashamed of that—my imagination can stretch wider than any one world—but there was one daydream, my favorite, that shames me to think about now. I loved it the best and still do. It's there deep inside me, and I have to struggle to keep it locked up like a wicked genie in a bottle, never again to be set free.

That winter, the Scheiners bought a country place up at Squaw Valley.

"It's got two bedrooms downstairs and another upstairs and a sleeping balcony and a deck all around the back and along one side, and it's all redwood and so beautiful. Just wait till you see it," Lolly said.

That was on the Washington's birthday weekend, and I was invited. We would ski all day and loll around the fireplace at night, drinking hot chocolate and talking. Lolly and her family all had skis and ski clothes, but she told me I could rent mine. I needed skis and boots and poles and ski pants. It would cost around twenty dollars. Mom said she couldn't afford it. I told Lolly I couldn't come.

"Why not?"

"I just can't."

"But you wanted to come. You were all excited about coming. Why did you change your mind all of a sudden?"

I made her promise not to tell anybody else and then I told her. She promised, but I knew she told her mother because the next day she said awkwardly, "My mother has an extra pair of skis and some extra ski clothes, too. They're big on her so they should fit you, and I know your shoe size is 7½, just like hers. So you won't have to rent anything."

I wanted to go. It was another daydream of mine— me zipping down the snowy slopes with the blue sky above me and the feel of the wind in my face. I knew it would be beautiful. I also knew that Lolly had spoken to her mother and somehow the extra equipment had been mobilized. Which left me two alternatives. If I accused her of telling her mother in spite of her promise, then I could maintain my pride and dignity. I also wouldn't be able to go. On the other hand, if I pretended to accept Lolly's story, I could go, but her betrayal would rankle.

Lolly made it easy by squeezing my hand and saying, "Oh please come, Pat. I'll have a miserable time if you don't come."

She gave me a third alternative, which was that of doing something for a friend—making a friend happy. I became the donor, she the recipient.

It never occurred to me then, but now I know how much Lolly understood people. I thought she was weak and hypocritical, but there was a larger reason that I couldn't understand at first. Lolly liked people and didn't want to hurt them—especially the ones she cared about. She'd change herself to make people comfortable. She knew how to do it, and it seemed to me, during that time, that she was sneaky and dishonest.

"They baby you all the time," I told her when we were up at Squaw. "Your mother's bad enough but your brothers and your father treat you as if you were younger than Joey, and you go along with it."

"It's because I'm the baby, and the only girl," she said, watching me uncertainly.

"But you're fourteen now. You're not a baby anymore. They treat you like you're a toy—a mindless plaything."

"No they don't. They're very proud of me."

"They're proud because you're so pretty and so feminine. At least, that's what they consider feminine—all beauty and no brains. And you play along with it. You act helpless and dumb. You pout and you squeak and you open your big blue eyes and act like those big smart males just know everything."

We were standing outside on the deck, just before dinner on the second day of our three-day weekend. It had been another frustrating day for me. Instead of flying down the snowy slopes as I had pictured in my daydreams, I had spent another day in the beginners' class, barely managing to move along, and hopelessly terrified of the lift. Lolly, who knew how to ski, went off for most of the time with her family, but had loyally checked in with me from time to time, supervising my clumsy attempts with infuriating cheerfulness.

All of my body ached—my shoulders, one hip on which I had fallen several times, and my thighs which were so deeply muscle-bound, I could scarcely move without wincing.

Lolly turned her head away and remained silent.

"Just because they're a bunch of male chauvinists doesn't mean you have to play the part of the dumb blonde," I snapped at her. "Don't you have any pride?"

Lolly faced me then. There were tears in her eyes, and she shook her head back and forth.

"Lolly," I said, "Lolly, don't cry. I'm sorry if I hurt you, but . . ."

"I don't know who I am," Lolly said. The tears were flowing down her face now. I looked at them in horror and didn't know what to say. What kind of a friend was I, anyway?

"Sometimes I feel so cornered," she said. "Sometimes I hate myself. Nothing goes right for me. I wake up and I think today is going to be different. I'll think of some other way, but it's always the same. I don't want it to be the same. I don't. But I don't know what I want."

"Lolly, Lolly," I said, putting out my hand. I'd seen Lolly cry lots of times. She was always a big crier, but this was different.

"I want to be somebody too. Greg and Michael—they're smart. They're going to be doctors. They know what they're going to be. And you know what you're going to be. But not me. And I want to be somebody."

"You are," I told her. "You are somebody. You're one of the nicest people I know."

"No!" she shuddered. "I don't want to be nice. I want to be special. I want to be me, but I want to be special too. I want to be able to do something really well. But I don't know what."

"You draw very well, Lolly, better than most people. . . ."

"No. Everybody tells me that, but that's not what I mean. I used to say I was going to be a fashion designer, but I don't want to do that anymore—but nobody hears me. Not my family, not you—not anybody."

"I hear you, Lolly," I said.

"No you don't," she wailed. "You think I'm a dope and a hypocrite because I try to get along with everybody, but I'm too mixed-up now to know what to do."

"I'm sorry, Lolly. I really am."

"I'm not like you, Pat, you know," Lolly said, wiping her face with her sleeve. It left a few shiny tracks running like ski trails across her face. "You're lucky!"

"I'm lucky," I repeated. "How can you say I'm lucky? You've got everything. You're the one who's lucky."

Lolly was watching me—not crying now—just looking me over as if she was seeing me for the first time.

"I guess I'm jealous of you," I muttered. "I guess I've always been."

"Of me?" Lolly squealed. "Oh, Pat, how could you be jealous of me?"

We kept it up after dinner and all through the evening and most of all when we were tucked inside our sleeping bags up on the balcony. It was easier to confess it all, whispering there in the darkness, not seeing each other's faces.

"I was always jealous of you," Lolly said. "You were so smart and so daring. All the kids were crazy about you and you could do anything you wanted. I always had to ask my mother for every little thing. I used to think how exciting it would be to live over a store and eat out of cans."

"And I wished I could be rich like you and have a family that always fussed over me and bought me clothes and presents the way yours always did. And your father—he looks so distinguished—your father, with his gray sideburns, and he thinks you're wonderful. Remember the time he took you to the concert?"

"No," said Lolly.

"It was a violinist, and you didn't want to go, and you had lunch, just the two of you, at a restaurant and . . ."

"I don't remember."

"He bought you a little blue-and-white china windmill filled with candy, and you broke it the next day in school, and . . ."

"Are you sure?"

"And see, you don't even remember it because he's always doing nice things for you. But I was jealous that you had a father like that. And now you turned out to be so pretty and you've become the popular one and the boys like you . . ."

"Oh, boys!" said Lolly. "But Pat, even though I was jealous, honestly, I was always proud of you and glad that you were my friend."

"Me too," I told her. "But Lolly, can I ask you something?"

"What?"

"You promise you'll tell me the truth?"

"I promise."

"Did your mother really have all those extra clothes and ski equipment?"

"Pat."

"What?"

"You promise not to get mad?"

"I promise."

"No she didn't. I told her, even though I promised I wouldn't, and she rented them for you."

"That's what I thought."

"And you're not mad?"

"No . . . and Lolly."

"What?"

"I'm sorry I made you feel bad. I don't really think you act like a dumb blonde."

"Oh yes I do," Lolly said cheerfully, "and sometimes that's the way I really am. But not most of the time. Not when I'm alone, and not when I'm with you."

"I guess I wasn't being fair to you," I told her. "But from now on I will."

We talked very late into the night. From time to time

one or the other of Lolly's parents yelled out for us to shut up, but we didn't until it was nearly morning. Next day, I finally managed to get myself onto the lift and to wobble my way down a small slope. The wind did fly in my face, the sky was blue above me, and Lolly stayed with me for most of the time. This was one daydream that came true, thanks to Lolly.

We were separated in my ninth-grade class picture. There are eleven of us in the back row, but only five of us are girls and there are six boys who are taller than me. Kenny Saxton is one of them. He looks like a telephone pole—very long, very stringy with wild, frizzy hair. My eyes blinked when the picture was snapped so I look half-asleep. Lolly is sitting down in the middle row, and Andy Lazlow is sitting next to her. His face is half-turned toward hers and they are both smiling at something he must have been saying. He is wearing a San Francisco Giants jacket, and he was the first of a long line of jocks drawn to Lolly. Ronny Cabell isn't in the picture because he moved to Fresno. I remained faithful to his memory, though—at least through most of the ninth grade.

Chapter 11

Mr. Evans listened to me. Most grown-ups don't like talking to teen-agers, much less listening. Sometimes they try to listen, but most of them drift off right when you're in the middle of something that's tearing you apart. You see them nodding at you, or making sympathetic clucking noises, but their eyes are glazing over with boredom.

Mr. Evans really listened. I told him everything when I was in the tenth grade—more than I even told Lolly. I could talk to him about my family. I could tell him how I looked at my mother sometimes, and a cool, precise voice inside my head said, "I do not like that woman."

He didn't tell me I had to like her because she was my mother. He didn't even say I should try to understand her because she'd had a hard life. He never said anything when I talked to him about my mother. He just listened.

When I talked to him about my father, he always tried to make a joke of it.

"Anybody who had a kid like you would run off," he said, or he called me "the greatest genetic mystery of the century."

I figured out that Luke had been born six months after they were married, and I told him so.

"Three months premature," he told me.

"Bull," I said. "But you didn't have to get married, did you? Nowadays, people don't get married just because one of them is pregnant. Mrs. Evans could have had an abortion or she could have . . ."

"But it was Mr. Evans's baby too," he said. "Remember that."

"My father didn't feel that way."

"We don't know how your father felt, do we? And in all fairness, he didn't know your mother was pregnant. But getting back to me, since you were kind enough to raise this most delicate question—no, we were not planning on getting married at that time. Meg was starting out in law school, and I wasn't ready for the domestic scene. At least I thought I wasn't."

"So?"

"I guess we both wanted the baby, and each other, too."

It wasn't a mistake. They were happy together and they adored Luke. He was three and a half now, spoiled rotten, and when he got sore he could scream until his face turned as red as his hair. But most of the time, he was a funny, noisy, affectionate little boy. I baby-sat for him just about every Friday or Saturday night and sometimes on Wednesday nights as well.

Mrs. Evans worked part-time for a public interest law firm, and she and Mr. Evans were debating whether or not they should have another baby.

"I think one-kid families are creepy," I told them. I was in on the discussions. "Most only kids I know are self-centered and obnoxious. Kenny Saxton's an only child. You remember him, don't you, Mr. Evans? He's not obnoxious, but nobody can stand listening to him. He has no sense of reality. He'll go on and on about fossils and never think to notice if he's boring everybody. His mother thinks he's the cat's meow. Besides, it's more fun with two or three in a family."

"More fun for whom?" Mr. Evans wanted to know.

"For the kids."

"But you and your brothers are always scrapping."

"Not always. But if I didn't have them, I'd have my mother all to myself."

"So you're saying poor Luke will have Meg and me all to himself and it would be much fairer if we produced another poor suffering victim to help him share the misery."

"Exactly."

Sometimes, if he and Mrs. Evans were going to be out late Saturday night, I'd sleep over at their house. In the morning, Luke and I would get up first and we'd mix up some waffle batter. Often, Mrs. Evans managed to sleep through the noise and the smells, but Mr. Evans, sooner or later, would come sniffing his way into the kitchen. Then the three of us would sit down at the table and eat waffles and talk and enjoy the lazy Sunday morning feeling. If we sat long enough, Mrs. Evans, her eyes puffy with sleep and her hair in jagged, red points, might stumble to the table and join us. It was a bright, colorful kitchen with a blossoming maple tree outside one window. I loved those Sunday morning breakfasts. I loved the Evanses, and sometimes I wanted time to stop and leave us there, the four of us, sitting forever around the pretty oak table. I can still smell the waffles in my mind and taste the melted butter mixed with the syrup. It is one of my favorite memories, before the daydreams started, and I am trying to fix it in my mind and let the others fade.

Mr. Evans was at me all the time when I started high school. Study! Study! Study! he kept telling me. Learn! Think! Read! Take this course! Take that course! Use your head! Don't waste your time!

I told him more about me than I told anybody else. But I didn't tell him everything. I didn't tell him how much time I spent twisting and turning in front of the mirror at home. Sometimes when the light was not too strong on my pimples, my skin glowed like deep ivory, and my dark eyes and hair cried mystery and romance. I used to wrap a red gold scarf around my neck and sling some of my mother's junk jewelry around my bare neck and slip on her slinky, low-cut, black shirt. I was beautiful then—as beautiful as Lolly, as beautiful as Helen of Troy or Linda Ronstadt. I preened myself before the mirror only when I was alone in the house. I lowered my eyelids and talked in a deep, breathy, sexy voice. I sidled up to the mirror and I rubbed up against my image. One day, I told myself, that image in the mirror will reveal itself to others as well as to myself.

"Study! Learn! This is the time you should be preparing for your future," said Mr. Evans, who evidently did not see in my face what I saw in the mirror.

None of my old friends were in my homeroom class

in high school. Lolly had fourth-period lunch and I had fifth. Sometimes a whole day could go by without our seeing each other. I didn't know most of the kids in my classes and, for the first time in my life, I felt shy and awkward. It didn't help that I took Mr. Evans's advice and studied and read and learned.

Lolly hardly ever studied. She had no time to study. She was too busy with extracurricular activities. She joined everything. She auditioned and was picked almost immediately for a part in the school musical that fall. She joined the cheerleaders and the band. Most of her afternoons were taken up with school activities. Whenever I did bump into her in the halls, she was always surrounded with at least one male in a letter jacket.

"Hey, Pat, wait up!" She'd talk to me in a fast, high voice, asking me where I was going, what I was doing that day—not really listening to what I was saying. She'd sling her arm affectionately across my shoulders or give me an overly enthusiastic hug. She'd be smiling at me, but her eyes would be flitting from one of her followers to another. She'd chirp on and on, in a stagy way. I knew she was playing to a larger audience now, and I resented being one of the props.

I told her so. We were riding home on the bus from school on one of her free days, the five of us. It was never just the two of us anymore, and she was asking me if I wanted to go see *The Sting* with her over the weekend.

"I'll go," said Eddie Baron.

"Oh you!" Lolly waggled her hand at him. "I didn't ask you."

Ted Sheriff and Cal Fitzgerald immediately offered themselves, and she was so busy giggling and flirting with all three of them at the same time that at first she didn't hear me.

"What?" she finally asked. "And the three of you shut up. I can't hear Pat."

"It doesn't matter," I told her. "You haven't heard me for a long time. In any case, I'm getting off here."

"But we're still a couple of blocks from your stop."

"No," I told her. "I'm getting off here, and don't bother waiting for me anymore on your free days. I'm going to be busy from now on."

Lolly came over to my house alone that weekend. She cried and I cried and she promised never, never to make me feel like a fifth wheel again. I promised not to be jealous, and by the following Saturday night, both of us had broken our promises.

Lolly knew I had a crush on a boy named Jim Lyons. He had taken Ronny Cabell's place. I used to watch him in my French class. He sat across the room and closer to the front, so I could look at the back of his head unobserved. What a head it was—all covered with soft, light brown hair that caught golden glints from the overhead light. And the shape of it! So fine and long and set so strongly on a brown, manly neck! I didn't know the front of his head as well as the back but whenever I did see it, I was enchanted by its large, hazel eyes and straight nose. Although he never spoke to me, and only nodded absentmindedly if we passed each other in the hall, I cherished the belief that he knew who I was and liked me.

Lolly arranged a double date. We went out to see *The Sting* the next Saturday night. She was with Eddie Baron and she asked Jim Lyons to come along for me. I can laugh now when I think of the hours I spent arched before my bedroom mirror. I forced Bobby and Joey to sit in the living room that afternoon and judge each outfit I tried on and paraded before them.

"On a scale of one to ten, boys, what do you think?"

"Three," said Bobby, about the new green sweater and jeans I was planning to wear that night.

"One," said Joey.

They disagreed on everything but finally, realizing that I would keep them there forever unless they could muster up some agreement and enthusiasm, they gave me a unanimous ten on my old pair of baggy striped overalls and tan San Quentin T-shirt.

"But I want to look sexy," I told them.

Then they started clowning around and making obscene remarks about my figure and falling all over one another. So I chased them, and ended up wearing the green sweater and jeans. I put on eye makeup seven times, using different shades of green, blue, lavender, and brown. I finally settled for black mascara with green eye shadow and a deep rosy tan lipstick.

"Nine and a half on a scale of one to ten—you are nine and a half or maybe even nine and three-quarters," I whispered to my image in the mirror. "You are gorgeous."

Maybe I was, but nobody else noticed. I didn't have a chance. Both boys were totally occupied with Lolly. After the movie, we drove in Eddie's car to Farrell's for ice cream. "What? What?" Jim kept saying every time I said anything. But he heard everything Lolly said even though she was sitting in the front seat. By the end of the evening, it had become a three-way conversation, with me smoldering silently and unnoticed in my corner.

"Never again," I told Lolly over the phone the next day. "I'll never go out on a double date with you again."

"But Pat," she said, "I could see Jim liked you. He told me you were the smartest person he ever met."

"Thanks a lot."

"And the nicest. I'm sure he said the nicest."

"Look Lolly, I've been hating you all night and I really don't want this beautiful friendship to end so let's just not—ever, ever again—go out on a double date."

"All right, Pat," she said meekly. "And you're not mad?"

"Sure I'm mad, and jealous too—but I'll get over it."

It was a glorious year for me and a terrible one, my first year in high school. I felt my mind opening up. I could understand so many new things—not only in math and science but in other subjects as well. Sometimes I got high on my own brain. I found myself judging my classmates, despising those who plodded along and those whose interests seemed low and unworthy. Teachers, for the most part, adored me, and I gloried in it.

At first, Lolly tried to include me in her activities, to give me a place of honor at her court. I'd see her talking and laughing with her friends, that eager, uncertain, "fat" look still there on her face, and she'd wave or motion for me to join her. But I needed my time and I didn't like her friends. Sure—I was jealous too. Sometimes we argued and stopped talking to each other. Sometimes I was lonely and that's when the daydreams really began.

In the yearbook, my picture appears only once—in the small individual pictures all the students took. I am wearing a white blouse and smiling a tight, superior smile. I look smart and unappealing. Not at all like the wild, glamorous creature that smoldered inside my mirror at home. I look like a brain, which I was. But there was so much more to me than showed in that picture.

Lolly is all over that yearbook, as she was in the others yet to come. She has her head down in her individual picture, and is looking out under slightly lowered eyelids with a sparkling, fetching smile. She is in white too but, where I look pure and sexless, she looks warm and luxurious. She is smiling out at you in many other places too—in the cast picture, with the cheerleaders, the band, and in many of the random photographs that are supposed to show life at school. There is one of her alone in the red-and-white outfit of a cheerleader, sitting quietly on a bench, another eating a sandwich in the cafeteria, another waving from the bus, another with Eddie Baron, standing on the front steps, another playing volleyball in her green-and-white gym suit. . . .

There is a piece of me in the chemistry lab, a piece of the back of me bending over a Bunsen burner, but nobody could really tell it was me.

I yelled a lot at Bobby that year and fought with my mother whenever we couldn't avoid confronting each other. Lolly and I drifted apart—but never all the way. Sometimes when it seemed our friendship was all over, she'd call and ask me to go shopping with her. Sometimes when I felt frightened and particularly lonely, I'd call her and we'd talk for hours on the phone. My feelings for her ranged from jealousy to superiority. I gloated one day when I saw her in school with a large, ugly cold sore on her mouth, but I snapped at Kenny Saxton when he called her a birdbrain. When Joey broke his hip, Lolly came down to the hospital with us and stayed with me that afternoon and evening, even though she missed a cast rehearsal and a date with Jeff Rivers, the quarterback on the varsity football team.

Chapter 12

"I've never been so happy in my whole life," Lolly said.

We were standing in front of my INSECTICIDES AND FRUIT FLIES exhibit at the science fair. Tacked to one side of it was a blue ribbon which had written on it in gold letters *First Prize.*

I was feeling pretty happy myself, and I turned, smiling, toward Lolly. Her eyes, however, were not fastened in admiration upon my ribbon or even upon me. She was smiling dreamily up at the ceiling, and I understood that my exhibit and my award had little to do with her joy.

"Who's the lucky man?" I asked lightly. I was too happy myself to brood over her lack of interest in the implications of my experiment. She *had,* after all, come to the museum to see my exhibit. She was interested enough, even though her questions were polite and perfunctory.

"Oh Pat!" She grinned at me, squeezed my hand, and pretended to admire my exhibit. "It's really sensational, Pat. What a lot of work you must have done."

"Not really. I . . ."

"And such an original project!"

"Not really original, but on a high-school level it is. . . ."

"And knowing how to handle all that equipment. You really are a wonder."

She grabbed me and hugged me hard. "I'm so happy you got first prize. I knew you would."

"Well, she *is* the prize pig of the bunch," said Mr. Evans. He was standing there, holding Luke's hand. "I always knew she'd win for that."

Luke pulled his hand away from his father's. "Do you keep that ribbon?" he wanted to know.

"Uh-huh."

"Can I have it?"

"Well, Luke, I kind of think I might like to keep it myself," I told him. He frowned at me and stuck out his lip.

"I won't be your friend anymore."

"Oh yes you will when you see what I've got for you."

"What?" Now he was smiling at me again.

"But if you're not my friend anymore maybe I won't give it to you."

"You promised, Pat. You told me last week you were going to have a surprise for me."

"Okay, Lookey Pooh, here it is." I pulled out a jar from one side of my exhibit, filled with about fifteen fruit flies. "I didn't need to use these guys so you can take them home with you if you like."

"And don't let them out," said Mr. Evans. "Thanks a lot, Madame Curie, I knew I could count on you to make my life uncomfortable."

Luke was watching his fruit flies, entranced.

"What do I feed them, Pat? What do they like to eat?"

"Spinach and spinach juice," said his father. "Just like you."

"I'm hungry," Luke said. "You said I could have a treat, Daddy. Let's get something to eat. Come on, Pat, you too." He tugged at my hand.

"I have to wait here," I told him. "You go. I'll see you later."

"You're sitting tonight, don't forget," he said. "Come on, Daddy."

"He's getting gray," Lolly whispered after they'd gone. "And he's so skinny and drawn. Doesn't his wife ever feed him?"

"They don't have that kind of marriage," I told her loftily. "She's getting quite a reputation in her field, and she's got other things on her mind besides worrying about what's for dinner. And besides, he's thin because he jogs every morning. He wants to be thin."

"He doesn't look happy."

"He is happy," I said irritably. "He's very happy. But he's busy too. He's an assistant principal now, and he's gone back to school to get his Ph.D."

"Who looks after Luke?"

"Mr. Evans's mother when they're both working. But each of them tries to spend a lot of time with him, and I sit for him a couple of nights a week."

"They ought to have another kid."

"What do you know?" I snapped at her. "Lots of

couples nowadays only have one kid. And why should Mrs. Evans be stuck at home? She's too smart to be a housewife. She's smarter than most people I know. She's brilliant. She . . ."

She! It was always She! I tried to stop myself, but more and more she was occupying my shameful daydreams. She, falling off a ski lift at Tahoe and dying of a broken neck. She, contracting viral pneumonia and dying—quickly and painlessly—but dying. She, walking down the street during a sudden earthquake and being flung to the ground and dying—without pain, of course. She—Meg Evans—brilliant, kind, and loving Meg Evans who was so good to me in real life. In my daydreams, she had to die.

Mr. Evans was on my neck all the time, pushing me to take harder and harder courses, more and more honors work. He never seemed to be satisfied with anything I did. He joked about my being The Prize Pig, but Meg Evans gloried in my award and the implications of my work.

"You've really demonstrated how ineffective and dangerous insecticides are in the long run by developing this insecticide-resistant strain of fruit flies," she said. "And then, Pat, my God, Pat, you've actually seen the workings of evolution under your hands in a matter of months. You're only sixteen, and just look how much you've accomplished."

She'd be watching me, her face loving and admiring, or she'd hug me so hard I could smell her warm, sweaty smell. And just that morning, maybe, I'd sent her to another death in my daydreams.

"She should stay home all the time with her kid," Lolly said.

"Don't be a dope," I snapped, and turned away.

"What's the matter, Pat?" she said. "Why are you mad at me?"

Why was I? It wasn't Lolly who kept having those homicidal daydreams. I swallowed down my annoyance and said, "I'm sorry, Lolly, but let's just drop the Evanses."

"Fine with me. I wanted to tell you something great that's just happened to me."

"Who is it?"

"Oh Pat, it's not a boy. No, I just got elected president of the Ecology Club."

"Ecology Club? I didn't even know you were a member."

Lolly giggled. "Well, I wasn't until a few weeks ago. Jimmy Ellison—you know him, don't you?"

"Little guy? Very pushy? Always running for some office or other?"

"Uh-huh. Well, he got me interested in the Ecology Club. It's true—I only joined because of him, but now he's lost interest, and Joany Chu quit as president, so they elected me."

"How many are there?"

"About five—and only three come to meetings, but I think I can round up a few more."

"I'll bet you can. With you as president, the membership should increase to include just about every male in the junior class."

"I don't discriminate," Lolly grinned. "I take seniors and sophomores too."

"What do you do?" I wanted to know.

"We recycle bottles and cans, clean up the campus, and sometimes work on the beaches on weekends.

Right now, we're studying ways to cut down on air pollution and conserve energy. I've been doing some reading on the nuclear power plants and how they contaminate the environment. I'm going to recommend that our club study this too."

"Very worthy," I said, "but how are you going to have time? You've got one of the leading roles in *Guys and Dolls*, you're on the dance committee, and you're still a cheerleader, and I don't know what else."

"I'm just going to have to cut down on my other activities," Lolly said, "because this is important. It's a funny thing, Pat, but I feel good about the Ecology Club, better than I've felt about anything else."

"That's nice," I said, watching a mother and her son as they stopped in front of my exhibit. I moved a little closer to them so I could hear what they were saying, but Lolly followed after me, and she was talking so loud I could only hear her.

"I mean, I'm doing something important. I really believe it matters. We have to protect our environment, not only for ourselves but for future generations too. It's like being part of another time. Like what we do now matters hundreds of years from now."

The mother and son moved off. Lolly's face was strained with seriousness. "You never sounded like this before," I told her.

She smiled. "Isn't it wonderful?" she said. "I really feel I'm doing something that matters now."

"It is wonderful," I said, thinking about my own experiment with fruit flies. "You're talking about being a part of the future. I kept thinking about Darwin's theory of natural selection all the time I was working on my experiment, and it was like I was linked to the past."

And I was. As much to the past as to the future. As much to my own past as to the pasts of famous, great scientists. Since seventh grade I had been moving—all the way out from rocket engines to telescopes to space. And now all the way back to microscopes and genes. What if my eyes had been blue? What if my own genes had been different? What if . . . ?

Lolly wasn't listening to me. Her face had that dreamy look I'd seen in so many different classrooms down through the years. So often it meant she was out of things. But not this time.

In the school yearbook, under the section on clubs, there is a picture of the Ecology Club with 27 members—mostly male. But this was only the beginning for Lolly. By the time we graduated, the club was to boast a record membership of 144 members—107 of whom were male. Even in our junior year, the club's activities began to flower. One of the random school pictures shows Lolly and a group of 11 or 12 other members picking up trash around the school, and another shot has her and Freddy Holtzman up on the roof of the boiler room, surveying a small solar-energy unit. Naturally there are shots of her in the school play, outside the main entrance, grinning over her shoulder at the camera, and one misty close-up of her with her head thrown back. I am in several pictures too, aside from my individual picture. In the clubs section, I am in the Chemistry Club and in the California Scholarship Federation. There is also a picture of Kenny Saxton and me—just the two of us—in the chemistry lab, blinking at the camera. It is on the same page with the picture of Lolly and Freddy Holtzman, along with four other pictures of assorted couples in different places and positions around school.

Kenny and I had drifted into romance. When and how it had happened, I can't even remember. Maybe it started on the bus rides to the science museum where I now worked along with Kenny on my free afternoons. Maybe in the chem lab at school where we both volunteered our time, or maybe because I was the only one who would ever listen to him talk about paleotaxonomy and he was the only one (outside of the Evanses) who listened to me talk about fruit flies.

Kenny was planning to study paleobiology when he graduated, and thought he might go to the University of Michigan. Right now I was fascinated by genetics but thought I should hold off before deciding definitely what field of science to specialize in. If it wasn't for Mr. Evans, I would have been satisfied going to San Francisco State College or maybe commuting to U.C. Berkeley. He kept after me to apply to M.I.T. or Stanford.

"You should," Kenny said. "You'd probably get in."

We were sitting in his mother's car one Saturday night after the movie. Every Saturday night we went out to a movie, sat and talked in Kenny's mother's car for about an hour, and then made out for twenty minutes or so. We seldom went out with other kids. Kenny was taking off his glasses now which meant we were about to begin the finale.

Not that I had anything against making out. In the darkness I couldn't see Kenny's long, skinny face or his bobbling Adam's apple, and I loved the warmth of his arms around me and the smell of his boy skin.

"Just don't get into any trouble," my mother kept yammering, "because I'm not going to get stuck taking care of you if you do."

She didn't have to worry. Her example shining before me helped. But also the two of us never got carried away. We hugged and kissed and touched—but that was all. After twenty minutes or so, I'd say, "Good night," and Kenny would say, "See you in the lab Monday," and that was that.

My real romance generally began after I came home from my date with Kenny. If my mother was out, I'd go into our bedroom, turn the lamp on low, and flirt for a while with my image in the mirror, as I'd been doing over the past few years. Then, I'd get into bed, turn out the lights, and think about myself in the arms of one movie star or another—Robert Redford, Paul Newman, Al Pacino. Sometimes I picked famous men in history—Charles Darwin, François I, Karl Marx. Shamelessly, I made love to any male who caught my fancy, but more and more now, I ended up in the arms of Mr. Evans.

I tried to stop myself. Not tonight, I'd tell myself weakly. Leave them alone tonight. But then it would begin. First, Mrs. Evans had to die. I'd hurry through that part, and then, slowly, deliciously, with infinite patience, I'd fill in every detail of the aftermath. How I was there, comforting him after her death, consoling Luke, offering my help, my untiring sympathy. How he came to depend on me, to need me, and finally—to love me. There were tears and sighs, smiles and laughter, and at the end, there I was, in his arms forever and ever.

Maybe the next day, I'd be sitting for them and Meg would say, "There's some cold chicken in the refrigerator, and I bought a quart of Swensen's bittersweet chocolate—that's still your favorite flavor, isn't it? And if you want to have a friend over . . ."

How could I do it? How could I keep killing her off

and making love to her husband in my daydreams without being overwhelmed by a powerful sense of guilt? I tried to make it up to her. I washed her dishes, even though she told me not to. I swept her floors. And many times I mended the tears in her shirts although I seldom bothered with my own.

Chapter 13

I could hear Lolly screaming as I rang the door to her house. It reminded me of old times.

"It's disgusting," Mrs. Scheiner said to me. "She's simply too old to act like this just because she can't get her way."

Lolly was down on the floor, kicking and yelling, "I will go! I will! I will!"

"You will not!" shouted Mrs. Scheiner. "And that's final!"

"What is it?" I addressed the howling heap on the floor, but Mrs. Scheiner answered.

"It's that demonstration against the nuclear power plant in Calistoga Valley. They're planning to trespass on the grounds and get themselves arrested."

I suspected that was what it was even before I asked. Lolly had been throwing all her energies into organizing a contingent from our school to join the demonstration. She'd even asked me, but I was taking a special course in genetics out at Berkeley and didn't want to miss any sessions.

"I am so going," Lolly screamed, raising up a wet, puffy, red face. "I'm seventeen years old and I'm old enough to make up my own mind."

"You'd never guess it from the way you're behaving. But listen to me, Lorraine, as long as you live in this house, you'll just have to go along with what your parents say. And we're not letting you go down there and get yourself arrested. If you want to help out by circulating petitions or writing letters to your congressmen—any legal activities . . ."

Lolly began kicking and screaming again.

Her mother's face was tight. "This comes of giving her so much freedom. I keep telling my husband—he's always spoiled her. She's gotten her way in everything. She can stay out as late as she wants. She has her own car now. She can bring her friends home whenever she wants. Nobody ever says no to her. And this is the kind of thanks we get when we try to stop her from getting herself thrown in jail with God knows what kind of people. . . ."

"Good people," yelled Lolly, "the best kind of people. People who care. People who do something. . . ."

"Now Lolly," said her mother in a restrained voice, "you certainly can't say your father and I don't care. We've given money and sent letters. You know Daddy has always been opposed to nuclear energy plants."

"But not when it means putting yourself on the line."

"Nothing is accomplished when an angry mob breaks the law. And people get hurt. And sometimes they get shot at. And we're not letting you go."

"Hypocrite!" Lolly shrieked. "You're trying to make me into a hypocrite too, but I won't, I won't. . . ."

"I don't know what's happened to her," Mrs. Scheiner said to me plaintively. "Ever since she got involved with that club, something's snapped inside her brain. And the kind of people she brings home these days . . ."

She inspected me like old times, her eyes silently traveling over my stained jacket, my crumpled jeans, my scruffy shoes. I could feel myself melting down under her gaze. But this time, I apparently found favor in her eyes.

"Why can't you be more like Pat?" she said to the yowling bundle on the floor. "She's smart enough not to get involved in a dumb escapade like this."

"But I'm going," I said.

Lolly stopped screaming and sat up, looking at me, her mouth open.

"And your mother approves?" Mrs. Scheiner asked coldly.

I knew what she was thinking about my mother so I said to her, "No, I don't think my mother exactly approves. But she won't stop me from going. She . . . she . . . lets me be. I'm glad I have *that* kind of mother."

Well, it was the closest I ever came to telling her off. That was another daydream of mine—telling Mrs. Scheiner off. Standing straight up under that scrutiny of hers and telling her off. It was the best I could do, but not nearly up to the scathing, cutting remarks in my daydreams.

I did it for Lolly but it didn't help. She was not one of the twenty-eight from our school who joined the rally that day in March in Calistoga Valley. Ours was the largest high-school group from anywhere in northern California—and it was all due to Lolly's efforts.

Mr. Evans drove down to pick me up at the juvenile detention center after it was over. He was fuming.

"You idiot kid," he yelled at me as we started back home. "How could you have been so dumb? Your mother said she didn't know you were going to get yourself arrested or she never would have let you go."

"She would have," I told him. "Only thing she's worried about is me getting pregnant, and I told her before I started out there was no danger of that."

"Look, smart ass, don't try to be funny with me. You could have gotten yourself killed."

"No I couldn't," I told him. "I had to go for non-violence training before they'd let me take part in this."

"But all it takes is one hot head and one cop with a gun."

"They had guns all right," I told him, "and they looked scary, but all of us were very polite and very careful. We just sat down in front of them when they told us to disperse, and later, we sang songs when they arrested us."

" 'We Shall Overcome,' I suppose," said Mr. Evans.

"Yes, but we have new songs too, like 'The Einstein Blues' and 'Radioactive Rock.' "

"You never said anything to me," he glowered, "because you knew I'd stop you from going. You knew I'd never let you go if you told me."

"But Mr. Evans, you told me yourself that you took part in all those peace marches and demonstrations during the Vietnam War. So why shouldn't I protest something that's wrong?"

"I never got myself arrested," he said, "and besides, I was an adult."

"Well so am I," I told him. "I'm seventeen—that's an adult, isn't it?"

He drove on silently awhile, and then said, grumbling, "It's because nobody sets any limits for you. Nobody stops you from doing whatever you want. You always get your way. It's wrong for a girl your age."

I giggled. He sounded a lot like Mrs. Scheiner. But I was enjoying his anger, basking in his concern. And the two of us were alone together, driving off somewhere in the night. . . . It was almost as good as one of my daydreams.

"And you must have missed at least two or three sessions of your genetics class."

"Four or five," I told him. "I had to drop out."

"That's just great," he said. "And you still haven't heard anything from Stanford or M.I.T. It would be just wonderful if they find out you're spending all your time getting into trouble instead of . . ."

The mood was broken. "Instead of learning, studying, reading," I finished it for him. "I know all about it. You've been telling me that ever since I've known you, but you've got to leave me be. You've got to let me breathe. I'm more than a student. I'm a person too. I've got feelings. I can't be studying all the time. There are things outside of books, Mr. Evans, even for me. Here I'm going to be a scientist, and you're yelling at me because I'm demonstrating against nuclear power plants—against how they foul up the air and the water and the bones of human beings. You can't only see the world through books. I'm never going to make that mistake again."

A few weeks later I was accepted into both Stanford and M.I.T. I heard a few days before the picture of the senior class was taken, out on the football stands. Lolly and I are together in that picture. We're sitting in the third row, slightly to the left, and the wind is whipping Lolly's long, blonde hair out to the side. She is dressed in yellow, and between her hair and her clothes, she is the brightest spot in the whole picture. I don't look too bad either, considering I am right next to her. My face is glowing from the wind and maybe the pleasure of the two acceptances, and my eyes look very large and bright. In the yearbook, Lolly was voted not only Most Beautiful, as you might expect, but also Most Anti-Nuke. I am Most Likely to Succeed and Kenny Saxton is Most Intellectual.

My mother didn't seem too impressed by my acceptances into Stanford and M.I.T., or my subsequent scholarship from M.I.T., which Mr. Evans persuaded me to accept. The only thing that really delighted her in my senior year was the thought of my prom. She kept talking about it, asking me for details, and, for the first time in ages, acted as if she really approved of me. We looked through the papers together, considered all the ads, checked for sales. We shopped at Macy's, The Emporium, and ended up buying me a deep orange low-cut gown with a sheer orange jacket at I. Magnin.

"It's so much money," I protested.

"Never mind," said my mother. "It happens only once in a lifetime," and she began talking about accessories.

Kenny and I broke up two weeks before the prom. I had been thinking about it for months, even before the rally at Calistoga Valley. I liked Kenny, but increasingly he bored me. What I didn't know was that I evidently bored him too. One Saturday night, instead of Kenny taking off his glasses for our twenty minutes of making out, he just looked at me and said nervously, "Pat, I've been thinking . . ."

"What?" I asked.

"I just don't . . . I mean, I like you a lot, Pat, and I always will, but . . ."

"I think I know what you mean, Kenny, and it's okay with me."

"You're sure, Pat? I mean if you still want to go to the prom . . ."

"To tell you the truth, Kenny, I really don't want to go."

"Neither do I."

"Great. So it's settled then?"

"See you in the lab Monday," he said happily.

The only disappointment I felt at first was that he had to be the one who broke up with me. My pride hurt. But my pride was nothing compared to my mother's. All she could think of was that I wouldn't be going to the prom. She didn't talk to me for days, even though I returned the dress and got her money back.

Lolly was going to the prom with Larry Koestler, the secretary of the Ecology Club. She had bought a pale blue silk dress that bared one shoulder. In those last couple of weeks before the prom, the school was filled suddenly with pairings—couples holding hands, laughing together in corners, sitting in groups all over the campus. Only me, it seemed, moved solitary through a world filled with twos. I felt lonely and sorry for myself.

That Wednesday night I was sitting for the Evanses.

Mr. Evans had classes and Mrs. Evans was at a meeting. Luke and I made cheeseburgers, played with his blocks, and watched TV. After I put him to bed, I began washing up the dishes in the kitchen. It was only about eight-thirty, but suddenly there was Mr. Evans coming through the door.

"You're early tonight," I told him.

"One of the teachers didn't show, so the class was canceled. How's Luke?"

"Fine. He fell off his bike, and banged his elbow, and he's got a cut on his chin."

"Sounds like a normal day. Is he sleeping?"

"I think so."

"Maybe I'll just peek in."

He came back, still on tiptoe, grinning. "I snuck in a quick kiss, and he mumbled, 'Hi, Mommy.'"

I began scouring the stove, trying to avoid looking directly at him. It was becoming increasingly difficult for me to feel calm when I was near him.

"And what's new with Cinderella?"

"Nothing much." I concentrated on the grease around the stove knobs.

"Has Meg told you yet?"

"Told me what?" I began cleaning off the front of the refrigerator.

"That she's pregnant?"

I turned around and faced him. "Pregnant?"

"Uh-huh. You see we took your advice. Baby's due around Christmas."

"That's wonderful," I said slowly.

"I think so too. You're going away, and Luke's growing up. I need somebody else to push around. A little girl would be just right. I could push a daughter around the way I always pushed you around."

"She's going to be lucky," I told him, "your daughter. And Luke's lucky too—lucky to have you for a father. I used to think about you and wish you were my father. You tried to be all along. You've helped me and you've been good to me and I . . . I don't want you to be my father. I want . . . I . . . I don't want to go away to M.I.T. I don't want to go away from *you*. I don't ever want to go away from *you!*"

And there I was, suddenly bawling away, just standing there with a wet sponge in my hand, bawling away. Mr. Evans put his arms around me, sponge and all, and held me, and patted my back, and stroked my head, and whispered, "There, there, Pat. There, there, darling. Don't cry."

I was in his arms for the first time, really in his arms—tight and warm against his chest, wonderfully close to him. His rough cheek pressed against mine— no man had ever held me like this before. Kenny didn't count. I loved it, and I rested my face on his shoulder and cried and cried until his shoulder grew wet under my face.

For a time, he patted my back and murmured comforting words. Finally he unfastened me—I didn't detach easily—sat me down, and stood looking at me. I waited for him to say something, but he didn't. I looked at him and he looked at me. It seemed to me that all my hidden, guilty thoughts now lay exposed before him. I felt ashamed, awkward, and stupid. What would he say? What could he say?

He was watching me nervously, I suddenly realized. He didn't know what to say. He needed help.

"You're going to tell me it's a good thing I'm going away," I suggested.

"I guess so," he said uncomfortably.

"That I need to broaden my horizons . . . that I'm just a little anxious about going to a strange place and meeting strangers, that I . . ."

"Pat, Pat," he said, trying to smile. "Little Pat . . ."

"Not so little," I told him. "I'm nearly five-seven and you're only five-nine. And I'm going to be eighteen in October."

He cleared his throat and tried again. "It's not easy growing up," he said, "but you won't have any trouble, Pat, and you'll be meeting all sorts of new people, all sorts of . . ."

"Don't tell me that," I said fiercely. "I'll never meet anybody like you. I can't meet anybody like you. There isn't anybody else like you."

There was nothing he could say that would make me feel better, but he was looking nervous again so I told him, "But I'm going. Don't worry about that, Mr. Evans. I'm going, but I'll be back Christmas, maybe summers. I'll be back."

"That's what I'm really worried about," he said, grinning again, and he reached over and tweaked my ear just like he always used to do.

By the time Meg arrived home, it was all over and we were joking around again. He just couldn't handle it, and I guess I couldn't either, so we tucked it away and hid it out of sight. It's all over, I told myself that night as I lay in bed. It's over. No more! Don't do it anymore! Just one more time, I pleaded, one last time—one for the road. You don't have to kill Meg off this time. Now that she's pregnant, you have to stop killing her off. But let me have this one last time with him, and I swear I'll never do it again.

So I had her disappear—carried off by some mysterious benevolent spirit. I didn't really have the time to bother with the details. I got rid of her—temporarily— just long enough for Jason Evans and I to have that one long, last lingering good-bye in each other's arms.

Chapter 14

I kept my promise, too. They've been away all summer, visiting friends in Spain, and they won't return until after I leave for school. Just as well! The baby will arrive around Christmas, the same time I come home for the holidays. I know they both want a girl, and I am trying not to wish too hard for another boy. I really want them to be happy, but I can't bear thinking about Mr. Evans with a daughter.

I received three cards from them. Mrs. Evans wrote the first two. *The Prado is a magnificent museum with some splendid Goyas. I'm popping more and more every day.* And *Luke misses home, pizza, and his favorite baby-sitter. So do I.* Does she know about me? I wonder. Did he tell her? I hope he didn't, but maybe it wouldn't matter even if he did.

The last card, which arrived earlier this week, said, *You must be busy getting set for your trip East. Don't lose your courage! Just in case I never told you, I'm very proud of you and looking forward to hearing from you if you have any time to write. Otherwise, I'll see you Christmas, of course.* It was signed *Love, Jason.*

Today, the day before I leave for Massachusetts, I spent with Lolly. She knows all about my feelings for Mr. Evans. I've told her everything.

"He's so old," Lolly said. "How could you love anybody that old? He's old enough to be your father."

"No he's not. Only nineteen years difference. What's that? Now I'm seventeen, he's thirty-six; but when I'm thirty, he'll be forty-nine. When I'm forty, he'll be fifty-nine. When I'm fifty, he'll be sixty-nine. We'll both be old then."

"Besides, even if he was free, you couldn't expect him to wait for you. You have four years of college ahead of you, and then if you go on to graduate school, which you'll probably do . . ."

I sighed and nodded. It *was* hopeless.

"But," Lolly said softly, "he always liked you best. Everybody knew that in third grade. You were teacher's pet in third grade."

"He liked you too, and he liked Kenny and Joany Sussman . . ."

"But you were always special to him."

"Do you really think so?" I asked hungrily.

"Oh sure, Pat. Look how interested he always was in everything you ever did. And how proud he is of you."

"Do you really think he's proud of me? No, really, don't say so if you don't honestly think so."

"He really cares for you. Even though he's married now and has a family, he'll always have a special feeling for you, always. . . ."

Lolly! All summer she'd been nursing me along, listening to me, comforting me—my dear, good friend Lolly, who had so many problems of her own.

"Have you told your parents yet?" I asked her.

"Not yet."

"What are you waiting for? You're moving out at the end of the month, aren't you?"

"Yes, but I can't throw everything at them all at once. First I had to tell them that I wasn't going to Harmond College in the fall. I wouldn't have gone there anyway—silly, snobby school to keep empty-headed girls out of mischief until they get married. Okay, I told them in June, so they had a month to get used to that. In July, I took the job chopping up vegetables and cleaning tables in Kelly's Delly. You remember they wanted me to work over the summer in Dr. Racine's office? Oaky, so that's blow number two. Now comes the biggie. I'm going to wait until I'm eighteen. Then I'll tell them."

"What do you think they'll say?"

"You know what they'll say. Mom will have twelve fits, and Daddy will talk to me in his special voice for little girls and retarded patients." She giggled. "But they'll get used to it. It's not like I'm moving far away—yet. I'll come home and have dinner a couple times a week, and call every day—at first. I don't want to hurt them."

"I think my mother is looking forward to my going. She doesn't say so, but I guess she thinks the boys will be easier on her. I just hope Bobby doesn't end up getting stuck with all the work. Joey is a lot like her."

"They're going to miss you a lot."

"I know, and I'm going to miss them too."

"But they're big boys now and so independent. I'm sure they'll manage."

"I think they will too. I'm not really worried about them—but Lolly, what's going to happen to you after you move out?"

"You know, Pat. I'm going to work for Kelly's Delly and share an apartment with Marcia James, and get really involved with the Anti-Nuke movement, and . . ."

"But what will you do about yourself? I mean, Marcia James, well she's a nice girl, I guess, but nothing much upstairs."

"You're really a snob, Pat. Do you know that?" Lolly snapped, her soft face reddening.

"Maybe I am," I said, "but Marcia's only interested in clothes and disco dancing."

"That's all *you* know about her," Lolly said. "Just because she's turned off on school and likes good times doesn't mean she's a birdbrain. She's a nice girl, a sweet girl—I like her a lot. And besides, she's the only one I found who's ready to share an apartment with me."

I remained silent.

"I mean," Lolly continued, "I like her a lot, but not like you, Pat. Don't be jealous."

I shrugged. "I'm not jealous."

"Sure you are, but don't be. You know I need to get away from home. I need some time to think about what I want to do with my life. I want to do something that matters, and right now what matters is getting away from home and being in on the Anti-Nuke movement."

"Okay," I said, "you know I think you're right, but don't stop there. Don't hide behind it."

"You know something, Pat," Lolly said, "I'm glad

137

you're going away. You're my best friend, but I'm glad you're going."

"You know something, Lolly."

"What?"

"I'm glad I'm going too. But scared. Aren't you scared?"

"Of what?"

"Of what's ahead. Of the changes. Of the things we don't know about."

"No, I'm not scared."

"You always were, when we were little. You were scared of everything. You were the biggest crybaby in the world."

"And nothing ever scared you."

"But I'm scared now. I'm scared of what's going to happen."

"I'm not scared, Pat."

"Everything might change. Maybe I'll come back at Christmas, and you won't even want to be my friend anymore. Maybe Marcia James will be your best friend. Maybe you won't even live here. Maybe I'll flunk out at M.I.T. Maybe Bobby and Joey won't be able to manage without me. Maybe Mr. Evans won't . . ."

"Pat," Lolly said quietly, "maybe it will be even better than it's ever been."

"Maybe so," I said.